MEN AND ANGELS

MEN AND ANGELS

BY THEODORA WARD

NEW YORK / THE VIKING PRESS

First published in 1969 by The Viking Press, Inc.
625 Madison Avenue, New York, N.Y. 10022

Published simultaneously in Canada by
The Macmillan Company of Canada Limited

Library of Congress catalog card number: 75-83233

Printed in U.S.A.

ACKNOWLEDGMENTS

Anthroposophic Press, Inc.: From *The Mission of the Archangel Michael* (1961) by Rudolf Steiner, Anthroposophic Press, Inc., New York.

A. & C. Black Ltd.: From *Camp Six* by Francis Sydney Smythe.

Collins-Knowlton-Wing, Inc.: From "In the Wilderness" from *Collected Poems of Robert Graves*. Copyright © 1955 by Robert Graves. Reprinted by permission of Collins-Knowlton-Wing, Inc.

Harcourt, Brace & World, Inc., and Faber and Faber Ltd.: From "Little Gidding" in *Four Quartets*. Copyright 1943 by T. S. Eliot. Reprinted by permission of Harcourt, Brace & World, Inc., and Faber and Faber Ltd.

Harvard University Press: From *The Poems of Emily Dickinson*, edited by Thomas H. Johnson. Reprinted by permission of the publishers and the Trustees of Amherst College from Thomas H. Johnson, Editor, *The Poems of Emily Dickinson* (Cambridge, Mass.: The Belknap Press of Harvard University Press). Copyright 1951, 1955 by the President and Fellows of Harvard College.

OCT 1962

The Hogarth Press Ltd.: From *The Book of Hours* by Rainer Maria Rilke, translated by A. L. Peck.

Houghton Mifflin Company: From *Life and Letters* by Emily Dickinson.

Alfred A. Knopf: From *Confessions of Jakob Boehme*, edited by W. Scott Palmer.

Cornel Adam Lengyel: For *In Memoriam: George Santayana.*

Little, Brown and Company: For "The Devil had he fidelity" from *The Complete Poems of Emily Dickinson*, edited by Thomas H. Johnson. Copyright 1914, 1942 by Martha Dickinson Bianchi. Reprinted by permission of Little, Brown and Company.

W. W. Norton & Company, Inc., and Insel-Verlag: From Rainer Maria Rilke's *Duino Elegies*, translated by J. B. Leishman and Stephen Spender; and *Sonnets to Orpheus*, translated by M. D. Herter Norton.

Penguin Books Ltd.: From *The Dead Sea Scrolls in English* by G. Vermes.

Princeton University Press: From *The Living Symbol* by Gerhard Adler, Bollingen Series LXIII. Copyright © 1961 by Bollingen Foundation, New York. From *Early Christian Art* by C. R. Morey (Princeton University Press, 1942).

Routledge & Kegan Paul, Ltd.: From *Experiment in Depth* by P. W. Martin.

Sheed & Ward, Inc.: From *Representative Medieval and Tudor Plays*, translated and edited by Henry W. Wells and Roger S. Loomis. Copyright 1942 by Sheed & Ward, Inc., New York.

The Society of Authors: From Dante's *Divine Comedy*, translated by Laurence Binyon.

The Society for Promoting Christian Knowledge: From *St. Patrick, His Writings and Life* by Newport J. D. White.

The Viking Press, Inc.: From "The Liturgy of Saint James" from *A Treasury of Early Christianity* by Anne Fremantle.

Zondervan Publishing House: From *Commentary on the Book of Genesis* by Martin Luther, translated by Theodore Mueller.

[v

PREFACE

The flash of an unexpected word crossing the field of consciousness can start a wholly new train of thought and even precipitate a course of action. The word "angels" came upon me in this fashion some years ago. I had just completed a piece of work that had left me with the appetite for creation still unappeased. Turning inward, I asked, "What next?" and to my surprise the answer was almost instantaneous: "Angels!" "Why?" I demanded, hoping to brush aside this intrusive word, which at the time awoke no warm response, but the seemingly irrelevant subject clung to me insistently.

I believe such happenings are not a mere matter of chance. They have antecedents, and they may have meaning that lies below the level of consciousness. I was forced to give attention to the idea of angels, and while thinking about them I recalled the effect upon me a year or two before, when someone had given me at Christmastime an angel decoration cleverly constructed of gilt paper. It was obviously a female figure, made with a flair for engaging style and artistically within the bounds of good taste. But the pertness of the little figure had produced in me a perceptible shock. Since childhood, when the Old Testament stories had introduced me to the awesome "angel of the Lord," I had given little thought to angels, having left them among the beautiful but outworn adjuncts of a set of religious tenets.

Other supernatural figures familiar to childhood, such as giants, gnomes, and fairies, had long ago passed into their proper place as folk myths belonging to my cultural background, without leaving behind an emotional residue. Why, then, did the Christmas angel give me the feeling that something deep within me had been violated? My reaction, I felt, could not be attributed wholly to an early association. Something basic must lie at the root of a concept that in spite of neglect and depreciation still had the power to disturb me. I began to see it as a living symbol of something significant in human experience. In view of the way it had presented itself, it seemed important to find out something about the history of the concept of the angel and perhaps to discover why it has persisted so long.

It was not until several years later that the way seemed open for me to take the journey through time that resulted in the writing of this book. The venture was without a definite goal, for it was undertaken less to prove a point than to look for whatever meaning might be found along the way. My exploration took me into fields of learning in which I could not claim even amateur standing. It led me into fascinating byways from which I had to retreat lest I lose the main direction in which I was heading. A variety of winged figures, such as celestial attendants on the gods of India or Greek figures of Victory crowning heroes, was rejected because it seemed necessary to limit myself to the Judaeo-Christian tradition. The natural place to start was the Book of Genesis. From there I took a backward look into possible sources in the ancient civilizations of Mesopotamia and then proceeded forward through the centuries to our own time.

The book does not come under the heading of angelology, which has to do mainly with doctrines concerning angels, and it has little to say about the curious beliefs and practices connected with the lore of good and evil spirits. Holding as firmly as possible to the idea of the angel as a messenger—which is, after all, the meaning of the word—I have made the link between man and God that it represents the center around which to gather my material. With this theme in mind, I have concerned myself chiefly with the spontaneous reactions of saints, seers, poets, and a few heretics, as well as with some of the popular views that have influenced art and literature. From the vast accumulations of religious writings, literary references, and representations in art that are available, I have used only such material as I could discover for myself or to which my attention was drawn by scholars who kindly suggested sources. In writing of angel appearances in the Bible narratives I have avoided interpretations based on any special system of theology or theory of scholarship and concentrated on the human aspects of the stories as shown in the texts.

In my wanderings through four thousand years I have surely missed much that might seem important to other people following a similar course. Readers may notice gaps and omissions, but I hope they may find a certain continuity in the development of the theme. The account of an expedition carried on from point to point without a map does not result in a complete guidebook for the territory covered, but it may suggest to others some fields of interest for further exploration.

CONTENTS

ILLUSTRATIONS

ILLUSTRATIONS

Two angels with the Tree of Life, from west façade of the Cathedral of St. Pierre at Angoulême.

Smiling angel, Gothic figure from Reims cathedral

MEN AND ANGELS

1 / ABRAHAM'S VISITORS

*The Angel of the Lord encampeth round about
them that fear him and delivereth them.*

—PSALM 34:7

The word "angel" presents some mental image to every heir to Western culture, whether of Christian or Jewish background. Not all, however, are aware of the frequency with which the word is used or of the long history that lies behind the concept of the angel. It has clung with great persistence to the body of basic patterns that furnish the background of the mind from generation to generation. It is as ubiquitous in the twentieth century as it was in the tenth, though it occupies a different place and is given less attention. Pick up almost any book in English, other than the purely scientific—presumably the same can be said of books in other European languages—and you are likely to find the word "angel" somewhere in the text. It is often used as a figure of speech to denote the ultimate in purity, innocence, or simple human kindness, but outside of the

[3

dogma of a few orthodox religions, the idea of the angel as the messenger of God has been generally relegated to the clutter of discarded superstitions. The awesome angel of the Lord encountered in the Old Testament has disappeared from the popular consciousness and given place to a variety of winged figures that would be unrecognizable to the psalmist who felt so sure of the protective presence of God's representative that it seemed to surround him.

Nowadays angel forms appear as trademarks for an assortment of commercial goods. Christmas cards display fantastic flying figures with trumpets or chubby winged children, who carry lighted candles or stand on sturdy feet with mouths wide open singing "Noël." From his stature as a prince of heaven the angel has diminished in the public eye to a mere decoration, but he is not entirely absent. The kernel may be missing from the concept, but the form has been kept because something in the recesses of the human mind still needs it as a symbol. The concept of the angel may indeed prove to have special meaning for a generation for whom science is paramount, since it springs from a part of human experience as yet barely touched by scientific thought. Quite apart from the works commissioned for modern churches, angels in recent years have begun to appear in the paintings and sculpture of a number of Jewish and Christian artists.

If you ask anyone to describe an angel, he is almost sure to mention wings as an identifying feature. Artists through many centuries have depicted these spiritual beings as winged and have made full use of the wings for their decorative effect. The association of wings with angels has been so usual that as late as the 1930s the *Shorter Oxford*

English Dictionary defined the word "wing" as "one of the limbs or organs by which the flight of a bird, bat, insect, angel, etc., is effected." The inclusion of the angel among the flies and sparrows might elicit a comment of a wholly different nature, but it also implies that, in the generally accepted view, wings are indispensable to a celestial being. In the earliest stories of angel appearances, however, wings were by no means essential, and they were altogether absent in most of the Bible passages on which the Judaeo-Christian tradition is based.

Every mythology contains winged beings. In the Eastern religions there are many minor gods and celestial attendants that fly. Since wings signify the ability to move in any direction, man, whose physical apparatus confines him to the earth, finds in wings a symbol of spirit. The bird, because it is at home in the air, takes on spiritual attributes, as we see in the hawk representing the Egyptian god Horus, in the dove descending on the head of Jesus at his baptism, and even in Shelly's skylark. Beasts of the earth, too, such as the Persian lion and the Greek Pegasus, have been given wings to symbolize their godlike powers. Folk tales not directly traceable to religious traditions also contribute their share of winged beings with supernatural faculties. The fairy godmother and her sisters are usually depicted with wings resembling those of a butterfly, and dragons and other monsters are equipped with gigantic bat wings or wings of some wholly fantastic form. It is not strange that the Christian artists, too, gave their angels wings.

What, then, does distinguish an angel from a fairy, a jinni, or a minor god? The concept of the angel is peculiar to the monotheistic religions, in which the immensity of the power concentrated in one universal god must somehow be channeled to reach the needs of man, as a great river may be diverted into a system of ducts to irrigate fields. The angel is a messenger, as the Greek word *angelos* and the Hebrew *mal'ak* both testify, who is sent from God to carry out the will of his creator. Messengers of the gods have a place in other religions, of course, but they are of a different nature. Hermes, for instance, whom we sometimes see fitted out with tiny symbolic wings on heels and hat, was a god in his own right, having attributes and activities of his own. The Hebrews thought of angels as having emanated from Yahweh himself. As his creations they were called "sons of God," and they represented him so completely that the voice of an angel was God's voice and the act of an angel was the act of God. Long before angels were represented with wings, their movements between heaven and earth were taken for granted. Heaven and earth in those days were considered parts of a unified whole, and there was no clear distinction between the natural and the supernatural. The sudden appearance of an angel where his presence was needed would have caused no surprise, and it was not necessary to inquire into his means of travel.

Mythology does not develop from concepts set forth by theologians whose concern it is to establish a reasonable system. It grows from the experience of men and women who become aware of phenomena and events for which they have no explanation. Whatever forms they may be projected into, myths all deal with life and spring from some need in the individuals who collectively are their source. Man is essentially the same as he was five thousand years ago, and his psychological experience today parallels that of his forebears, though his conscious attitudes have changed. The figure of the angel answers a need men have for an intermediary between themselves and the unknowable, immeasurable, and transcendent force they conceive of as in charge of the universe.

The idea of the celestial messenger does not merely represent the fulfillment of a wish, conscious or unconscious. It also offers an acceptable explanation of certain psychic phenomena to people who arrive at their perceptions through symbols. Certain persons through the ages have recorded experiences in which they had intimations of the presence near them of an entity that was felt rather than seen. This can happen quite as well in the twentieth century A.D. as in the twentieth century B.C., and it does not necessarily occur to those with a leaning toward mysticism. Sometimes, when a dangerous situation or a strong emotional upheaval has pushed a person beyond the limits of his usual state of consciousness, he becomes aware that the ego he is familiar with does not stand alone. Something else is there that he cannot explain in rational terms. The presence seems to be entirely separate from himself, and usually it has a beneficent effect, either comforting and sustaining or challenging and stimulating. The experience is felt as an encounter with a superior power.

When a highly intelligent, well-educated, and rational-minded American woman who is not an adherent of a traditional religious faith tells you that she has seen an angel, you cannot dismiss her statement as a mere figure of speech. At a crucial time in her life, such a woman told me she was so torn by inner conflict that she felt emotionally paralyzed and totally unable to make the necessary choice between two courses of action. As she sat, fully awake, in a state of agonizing suspension, feeling that her vital force had been withdrawn, she suddenly saw before her, standing in the room, an angel who held out his hands to her as if to offer help. Immediately the fearful tension loosened and the answer to her problem came clearly and authoritatively, as from a power beyond her knowledge or control.

The form of this woman's vision—the angel in shining white robes—was no doubt influenced by her knowledge of Christian art, but the feeling of having had an encounter with a being of a wholly spiritual nature, who was able to break her psychic paralysis, was strong and real. In just such a simple and direct way occurred the meetings between men and angels recorded by the writers of the books of the Old Testament. Something of a numinous nature had happened in the woman's inner world, and the vision she saw corresponded to this.[1]

A much more common occurrence that can also be interpreted as an angel's visitation is the sudden consciousness of a mental image or idea that seems startlingly new and of particular importance. Where it came from and who put it there are questions that naturally arise. If the idea is one that brings illumination or seems to offer guidance for action in a new direction, if it assuages the pain of an inner conflict or gives relief from anxiety caused by outer problems, it may be felt as the direct intervention of a supernatural being.

Not much attention is given to this aspect of the angel theme in reference books, which are more concerned with outlining the beliefs held by the adherents of religions than with seeking the origins of those beliefs in the human beings who formulated them. *The Jewish Encyclopedia* does suggest that it is an open question whether the concept of the angel can be traced to the deification of forces of nature in earlier religions or whether the idea of the angel fulfilled a psychological need for a mediator between man and God. If the history of religion follows the history of man himself, why is it necessary to choose between these two lines of inquiry? Why should not both be followed until, far back in ancient times, they meet in man's earliest attempts to explain his universe? Long before the religion of the Hebrews developed, their ancestors had shared beliefs out of which grew also other religions. They must have carried with them into their new faith a great many traces of the earlier nature worship. The gods of the earth, the rain, and the wind may easily have been transformed through the centuries into the angels who carried out in their specific duties the will of the supreme god. Any attempt to trace the immediate antecedents of the angels of the Hebrews must be purely speculative, but it enriches the background of the Bible stories to connect them, however tenuously, with the life and thought of the centuries that preceded the time of the patriarchs.

The monotheism of the Hebrews did not blossom full-grown under the hand of Abraham, but, like other human developments, was of slow growth. The persistence of earlier practices can be seen in the Genesis stories. Jacob's dearly loved Rachel committed the sin of carrying off the images of the household gods when she left her father's house to follow her husband into Canaan. Although the early Hebrews worshiped their tribal god to the exclusion of all others, they recognized the existence of those of

[9

other nations in the form of demons. If they lived, as the Bible says, at Ur, the great Sumerian capital, before the migration to Canaan, they must have been closely associated with the religion that permeated every phase of life in that rich and already ancient city.

Several universal symbols appear in the remains that have been excavated at Ur. The Sumerians pictured a spiritual world consisting, in early times, of three heavens—and, in later times, of seven. In the highest heaven were kept the bread and water of eternal life, under the protection of the most high god, An, from whom all the others were descended. A stele found at Ur shows a winged figure descending from heaven to pour the water of life from an overflowing jar into a cup held by the king. Some scholars have spoken of this as the earliest representation of an angel. As background for the conception of the angel found in the Old Testament, however, an entirely different source is suggested by the carvings on the cylinder seals, of which a great number have been found in the Sumerian remains.

The seals were evidently in common use, as signatures of individuals, for several centuries. The designs carved on them are seen to have developed from simple geometric patterns to elaborate depictions of scenes and events. During the third dynasty of Ur, closest to the probable time of Abraham, one theme predominated, though no two seals are identical. Most of them consist of three figures, one seated and two standing. Scholars believe the seated figure represents a god, to whom the owner of the seal is being introduced by an intermediary. As often as not, he is led forward by the hand, and sometimes the action of the figures gives the impression that he is reluctant or fearful—an attitude that no doubt adds to the stature of the god as an object of awe.

At this time in the history of Ur every house of any consequence appears to have contained a small chapel. Since each family had its tutelary god, it is natural to suppose that it was he who acted as mediator in the meeting of man and god. The god is physically present and has the appearance of a man, as does the assisting figure. It is not a long step from such a scene, in which gods and men walk side by side, to the early Hebrew narratives in which Yahweh is intimately associated with his people and the angel of the Lord is scarcely distinguishable from his creator.

Nearly two thousand years after the time of the migration, probably late in the first century of the Christian era, a small band of Christians received a letter of exhortation from someone who wrote with authority but whose identity is uncertain. Near the close of the Epistle to the Hebrews, in which the writer has shown how the whole course of Jewish religious history has led up to and been fulfilled in the gospel of Jesus Christ, he reminds his friends of some of the marks of Christian living. One of them is hospitality to strangers. It is not merely as a matter of simple courtesy or for the sake of human kindness that the Christians are urged to open their doors and their larders, but because "some have entertained angels unawares." It is an arresting thought that the passing stranger should be regarded as potentially a messenger of God and as one who may bring far-reaching results in the lives of both the host and the guest, giving to each encounter a heightened atmosphere and linking man to man in the recognition of the values in each.

The Hebrew Christians to whom this admonition was given, familiar as they must have been with their ancient literature, would have understood the reference. Their ancestor Abraham set the pattern for them when he ran from the door of his tent by the oaks of Mamre to receive three men whom he saw approaching. The writer of the story in Genesis lets the reader know immediately that this visit is from Yahweh. It is not clear, as the narrative progresses, at what point Abraham himself becomes aware of the identity of his visitors. It is soon apparent, however, that Yahweh himself is present. The other two persons appear to be his attendants, and this is borne out by the account in the next chapter of the arrival of the *two* angels at Sodom, which Yahweh has decided to destroy.

The Lord himself remains with Abraham, to reveal to him his intentions, and Abraham is able to intercede successfully on behalf of his friends who live in the doomed city. In this part of the story he appears to know who his visitors are, but certain gaps make one suspect that the writer has worked together several earlier versions of the legend. These slight lapses, however, do not detract at all from the happy picture the story gives of Abraham's spontaneous greeting to the three strangers and the details of his entertainment. There are no wings or shining garments in the picture, no trumpets or clouds of glory—just three men sitting under the oaks while their host stands beside them to superintend the serving of the meal of tender veal, freshly baked cakes made of the finest flour, milk, and cheese. We are told that "they did eat"—a touch that indicates how completely the celestial figures had assumed human form. It was not until the feast was over that the guests gave their message to their aging host, foretelling the birth to his wife, Sarah, of a child who was to carry on his line and whose descendants would become a great nation under Yahweh.

The story of Abraham's three visitors is not the first account of angel visitation in the legends of the patriarchs, but its graphic description of the warmly human scene has made it a favorite subject for artists. Christian painters especially used it often in times when entertaining strangers had become a custom in the monasteries. A legend of Gregory the Great in the sixth century seems to reflect the view that ordinary guests may turn out to be angels in disguise. After he became pope, Gregory once invited twelve poor men to dinner but found a thirteenth present, who partook of the meal with the rest. He appeared sometimes young, sometimes old. After dinner Gregory took the visitor by the hand and led him to his own room, where he asked his name. The thirteenth guest then revealed that he was an "angel of God" and that it was he who had appeared to Gregory years before in the guise of a shipwrecked mariner. At that time Gregory, then a poor monk, had given his destitute visitor all he had—a silver dish in which his mother had been accustomed to send him food. From that day, the angel said, God had destined him to become pope.[2]

By Gregory's time the angel had assumed a definite place and nature in the Christian conception of the spiritual world, but back in the age of the Abraham legends it was not always easy to separate the messenger from God himself. The narratives state that at least once Abraham met Yahweh face to face when he made the covenant that established him and his descendants as the chosen people. In the series of events that led up to this climax there is first the simple statement, "Yahweh said unto Abram"; then "Yahweh appeared unto Abram"; the third time, the narrative says, "the word of Yahweh came unto Abram in a vision," and later in the same episode "a horror of great darkness fell upon him," out of which God spoke again. Finally we read, "Yahweh appeared unto Abram and said unto him, I am God Almighty; walk before me and be thou perfect. . . . And Abram fell on his face: and God talked with him."

In the midst of the account of Yahweh's successive appearances to Abraham, another story is interpolated in which the word "angel" occurs for the first time in the Genesis text. The story of the lowly woman who was to bear Abraham's first son shows angels in a wholly different aspect from the one her master was soon to see. If anyone needed angelic help, surely Hagar, the Egyptian maidservant, did, for she seems to have had little sympathy from the human beings who were primarily responsible for her sufferings. Hagar must have had some acceptable traits, or she would not have been the one selected by her childless mistress, Sarah, to bear her husband a son. Her sudden accession to power, however, when she became pregnant, brought about a change, and the arrogance with which she taunted the older woman drove Sarah frantic. The punishment Sarah imposed on Hagar for her presumption, administered with Abraham's approval, was cruel enough to cause her to run away and face unknown dangers in the wilderness. No harm overtook her, however, for the story says, "The angel of the Lord found her." We are not told whether she actually saw the angel, but, lonely and disgraced as she was, she knew that she had been found by him.

The sense of being sought by a power greater than oneself is an essential part of the experience of angel visitation, and Hagar named the spring by which she was found "the well of the living one who seeth me." Armed with the knowledge that even she, a slave girl, was watched and protected, she was able to return and face the situation from which she had fled. Hagar's troubles were not yet over, for when her son, Ishmael, mocked the baby Isaac, the son miraculously born to Sarah in her old age, choosing the most inauspicious time, the feast day in Isaac's honor, both mother and son were dismissed to fend for themselves.

This time the hand of God is seen working things out on both sides in the clash of personalities. To Abraham, who was at first grieved at Sarah's request that the concubine and her son be sent away, God again spoke directly, assuring him that he had a plan for Ishmael as well as for Isaac and that the two were to be the progenitors of separate peoples. To Hagar, the angel of the Lord again brought comfort and practical assistance. When the water in the bottle Abraham had given her was gone and she was helpless to relieve the suffering of her child, the distressed mother cried aloud. Then "the angel of the Lord called to Hagar out of heaven . . . and God opened her eyes, and she saw a well of water; and she went and filled the bottle with water and gave the lad drink."

Some of the stories in Genesis are pieced together from different sources, but this one is a complete unit taken from a Hebrew text which is thought to be one of the earliest. Here is surely the first expression of the idea of the guardian angel, which was to become the most popular belief concerning angels among the Jews and the Christians. The angel of the Lord is still identified with Yahweh himself, but he is a manifestation of God's mercy shown in a form suitable for the person who is to receive it.

The different aspects of the divine voice become confusing in the account of Abraham's preparations to offer his beloved son Isaac on the altar of Yahweh. Here the voice of command seems to be working in opposition to the voice of mercy. It was Yahweh himself who told the devoted father to sacrifice his son, but it was the angel of the Lord who stayed the hand that already held a knife in readiness. All the steps so far had been taken in response to the inexorable god, whose ways were not to be questioned. When the altar was finished and the wood laid upon it, the young boy bound and the knife in the father's hand, the voice that came from heaven was the voice of the angel of the Lord, calling Abraham's name, not once but twice, as a person does when the call is urgent. "Abraham, Abraham," he said, "lay not thy hand upon the lad, neither do thou anything unto him."

Abraham's response is not given in words. Instead we are told that he looked around him. What he saw had been there all the time, but he had not seen the ram caught in the bushes, because it was behind him. Up to now he had blindly followed what he understood to be God's will. Human sacrifice was still practiced among the neighboring tribes, and Abraham's devotion to his own god was greater than that of the Canaanites to theirs. The Jews' religion took a step forward in this dramatic change in the value placed on human life. Not only was the angel of the Lord the manifestation of God's mercy; in this story, and in instance after instance in other stories of angel visitation, he represented the coming into consciousness of something new, marking the beginning of a new phase of growth.

In spite of his miraculous escape from death, Isaac himself seems to have been largely occupied with the practical affairs of a man of wealth, and though the Lord is said to have directed him, there are no records of his having received angel visitants. His son Jacob, however, a striking character of mixed high and low motives, was particularly subject to experiences with angels. The Abraham narrative shows angels only as attributes of Yahweh, acting in direct relation to certain individuals. New aspects of them are seen in the stories of Jacob, where they appear in visions. Here they are presented as separate entities, sometimes acting without any reference to the person seeing them. The first of these, the dream that came to Jacob on his way to find a wife in the land of his mother's people, showed angels, quite unconcerned about him, ascending and descending the stairs to heaven. To the people of his time Jacob's "ladder" was not a fantastic idea, for the Mesopotamian religions had always assumed there was one place where such a connection between heaven and earth was made. The gods in the temples dwelt in an upper chamber and on certain occasions came down to receive homage from their worshipers. Jacob's dream makes the anthropomorphic nature of the early angel image clear. Even though later Christian painters have usually given Jacob's angels wings, it is clear that they did not fly but walked up and down and were constantly coming and going on their errands to men. In the decorations of the synagogue at Dura-Europos, painted two hundred years after Christ, they are distinguished from ordinary men only by the court costumes they wear.

Jacob had a second vision twenty years later, as he was returning to Canaan after his long sojourn at the house of his uncle Laban. What he saw we can only guess, for the narrative is condensed into a single short sentence: "And Jacob went on his way, and the angels of God met him." No action on either side is mentioned, and no hint is given of what the experience meant to Jacob, whether he felt supported or intimidated by the appearance of the heavenly host. He named the place where it occurred Mahanaim, which means two hosts or companies, simply giving recognition to the fact that on one side was his own company of human beings and on the other, the company of God.

This vision may have seemed entirely impersonal, but it was a prelude to the great crisis in Jacob's life, when he was to face a crucial test. As he journeyed with his two wives, their children, servants, and his rich flocks and herds, he approached the territory of his brother, Esau. The deception with which Jacob had deprived his brother of the paternal blessing had left him with a well-justified fear of the man he had wronged. And now he could not avoid a meeting.

The dual character of Jacob comes out in the preparations he made for the meeting. Contriving to save himself by cunning, as he had always done, he sent messengers ahead to announce his coming, separated his herds into groups so as not to show all his strength at once, and sent one company ahead with substantial presents of sheep, goats, cattle, camels, and asses. It was not until he had made all these arrangements that he prayed earnestly to God, confessing his unworthiness and asking for help. Using both his wits and his faith, however, did not bring assurance of success. Help came in an unexpected form, for the schemer had to wrestle all night with a superhuman assailant. Having sent his wives and children away also, he was alone to face his guilt and his fear when the nameless "man" attacked him. The fight seems to have been a test of endurance in which he proved his ability to stand up against a superior force, even though he was hurt in the struggle. Tradition holds that Jacob's opponent was an angel, but the story in Genesis does not use the word. Jacob, according to Genesis, said that he had seen God face to face and, in spite of the awesome experience, was still alive.

There are many mythological stories of such struggles between a man and a god, in which the man wrests power from his divine opponent. The story of Jacob is similar in form but different in conclusion, because he does not emerge as a victorious hero. The fight was a draw, neither victory nor defeat, but having endured until he recognized the nature of the force that opposed him, Jacob obtained a blessing from his assailant. According to Jewish tradition, a blessing has an actual effect on the future of the person receiving it; and in the experience of life, the outer results of such a struggle as Jacob sustained often reflect the change it has wrought within the person who has endured it.

When the meeting with Esau took place, Jacob encountered no hostility, only brotherly love and generosity. Either the angel's blessing had worked a miracle, or Jacob's fears had been based entirely on the unadmitted guilt of twenty years. He went his way with a new name—Israel, the contender with God. A new name signifies a new person, and the subsequent narrative shows no sign of the schemer in Jacob, only the love of a family man and the wisdom of the leader of a tribe.

The adventures of the Israelites continued to include the presence of angels on many important occasions; but in the account of the sojourn in Egypt, the persecutions and the plagues, the deliverance and the wanderings in the wilderness, the wonders are said to have been performed by the Lord himself. God spoke directly to Moses, who, after seeing the burning bush, did not need any further proofs of the divine will. This greatest of all the Israelites seems to have taken on the role of the angel of the Lord himself, acting as intermediary between Yahweh and his people. An angel had a prominent part to play, however, in an episode that occurred as the children of Israel drew near the Promised Land. Perhaps there are certain people—though not necessarily all of the same type—who sense the indirect approach, or who function only on a particular level of consciousness. This was indeed the case with Balaam, to whom the divine voice could speak only through his animal companion.

The story of Balaam's encounter with an angel is only a small part of the narrative concerning him, but it is the only part that most readers recall. Almost everyone enjoys a good animal story, and the lowly ass has usually been held in affection, for human beings attribute to it both humility and stubbornness—qualities in which they often see themselves reflected. It may be because of its meditative expression that the donkey has also been credited with clairvoyance, though anyone who is acquainted with horses or dogs has noticed the uncanny awareness they too sometimes show of things unseen or unheard by their human companions. In any case, the example of the animal's obedience to instinctual patterns occasionally serves to restore balance to men and women who become inflated with their own superior knowledge and ability to reason. When the human mind begins to assume a godlike attitude, something is likely to happen to bring it back to the common level of natural law it shares with other living creatures. This is what seems to have occurred in the Balaam story.

Balaam, a renowned prophet and sorcerer, who was not one of Yahweh's people, was said to have come from Pether on the Euphrates, though it seems doubtful that he could have traveled on an ass the four hundred miles from that city to Moab near the Jordan. Balak, king of the Moabites, had sent for him to come and use his powers against the threatening horde of Israelites who had come up from Egypt and overrun the Jordan valley. Balaam was to be Balak's secret weapon against a potential enemy who outnumbered him. To send for magical help from such a distance shows both the extent of Balak's fear and the importance accorded to the effect of an authentic curse.

Complications in the text of the narrative as it appears in the Book of Numbers make the sequence of events hard to understand, for it seems to be made up of two versions that come to similar conclusions, though by different means.

When they are read in continuity, Yahweh is first seen entering into a compact with Balaam to go on the journey but to speak only the words God gives him. Later, however, Yahweh becomes angry with him for having gone. Balaam's own attitude is confused with that of the editors, whose motive is to glorify Yahweh and declare the greatness of the tribes of Israel. The episode of the ass and the angel may be an interpolation from another source, but it is so complete in itself that it can stand alone, as it does in the mind of the reader. It contains the kernel of meaning in the story and has the mythological quality of closeness to life. Humanly speaking, it is an account of an important man humbled and brought to see the truth through the agency of the beast of burden that hitherto has obeyed his will.

It was the ass that first saw an angel blocking Balaam's path. The particularity with which the animal is spoken of as "she" strengthens the mythic quality of the story, for the feminine is universally understood to represent the unseen, instinctual side of life. The Jewish religion is so overwhelmingly masculine that the introduction of the feminine element is especially striking.

As in many good stories, the action had to occur three times before it became effective. Twice the ass was forced to disobey her master in order to evade the angel with the sword, whose presence made it impossible to proceed. She was severely punished for leaving the road and for crushing Balaam's leg against a stone wall. The third time Yahweh himself came to the assistance of the outraged animal by opening Balaam's ears to her speech and his eyes to the supernatural presence before him. Overcome with awe, and in deep humility, Balaam offered to give up his plans and return whence he had come, but the Lord told him to continue and to speak only the words he would give him. The words he spoke were not those of a curse but of praise to Yaweh and blessing on the children of Israel. He had been brought to recognize a power greater than his own.

The angel of opposition whom Balaam met carried a sword; so did the prince of Yahweh's host who appeared before Joshua as he approached Jericho. But the angel who called Gideon, the son of a poor farmer, from the threshing floor to lead his people against their oppressors, the Midianites, carried only a staff, the peaceful instrument of the shepherd. Balaam was to be humbled and taught to obey, Joshua was instructed in tactics of warfare, but Gideon was to be raised up out of his humility and given confidence in himself and in Yahweh's leadership. The angel's staff proved also to be an instrument of divine demonstration, for when Gideon brought an offering of food to his visitor, the angel touched the meat and the cakes with his staff and they were consumed by fire as a sign of the presence of the Lord himself. The sword and the staff both remained as symbols in the hands of angels well into Christian times.

Aside from the angel who fed the prophet Elijah when he fled for his life into the wilderness, there are few references to angels in the books that carry the history of the Hebrews up to the time of the destruction of Jerusalem and the Babylonian captivity. When they are mentioned, it is usually in a figurative sense, as when "the angel of death" destroyed ninety thousand people in the time of David; or sometimes angels appear as visions, as when Elisha saw the armed hosts of God with chariots of fire outnumbering the Syrian army that encircled him. Angels are not so often instruments of the direct intervention of God, but are seen as heavenly hosts in a separate world. The sacred poems and hymns that constitute the Psalms allude often to angels, their nature and their duties in relation to men, always in a general sense and with poetic feeling. The time was coming when the idea of another world was to take a more definite form in the minds of the Hebrews, through the visions and speculations of their prophets and seers.

2 / THE COURT OF HEAVEN

Rank on rank the host of heaven spreads its vanguard on the way
As the Light of light descendeth from the realms of endless day
That the powers of hell may vanish as the darkness clears away.
—LITURGY OF SAINT JAMES

There are two distinct ways in which people have thought about angels. Either of them can be followed quite consistently, for, although they have long been associated in men's minds, they really stem from different sources. The first is an earlier line of thought than the second, and springs from a desire to describe events that have a numinous quality. In this way, the angel is seen as an aspect of God in direct relationship to men. In the second way, angels inhabit a spiritual world completely apart from man. This other world, gradually developed by the visionary minds of prophets, seers, and teachers of the Hebrew people, became a magnificent concept. In Christian times the picture was to undergo some changes at the hands of the

Fathers of the Church, but essentially it was to remain the same in its broad outlines for many centuries.

So far we have approached the subject largely from the first point of view, but in order to follow the theme of what angels have meant to people through the centuries, we must first catch a glimpse of the Jewish heaven as it took form and grew in the minds of mystics and scholars and was recorded mainly in Jewish literature other than the books of the Bible.

The early documents that make up the Pentateuch refer in several places to "the hosts of heaven," though it is sometimes hard to distinguish the army of God from the multitude of stars in the sky. This is not strange, since the Hebrew inheritance from the past included impressions of the divinity of the sun, moon, and stars, and contemporary religions continued to worship deities that were associated with the heavenly bodies. In the language of poetry it does not seem important to distinguish between the visible celestial pattern and the anthropomorphic picture of a supporting multitude of beings that surround the invisible God. The development of a cosmology out of these and other sources came gradually; its main structure was built and elaborated upon during and after the fall of Jerusalem to the Babylonians, and the consequent years of exile. Mingling, as they were forced to do, with other peoples, the Jews were inevitably influenced by the cultures of Persia, Babylonia, and Greece.

The disaster that overtook the Hebrews at that time, with the disruption of their tribal life, brought forth many spontaneous outbursts in the form of dreams and visions recorded in poetry and prophecy. Their kingdom on earth was crushed, but a kingdom of heaven was projected in its place. The splendor of the court of Babylon, under whose power the exiles lived, was utterly eclipsed in their minds by the glory of the court with which the one true God, the God of the Hebrews, was surrounded. During the succeeding centuries this picture of the spiritual world became more explicit and detailed, but it was never given official form by the rabbis. Ancient tradition depicted three heavens; the count later increased to seven, which became the most generally accepted number, though there was some pre-Christian authority for the nine heavens which Dionysius the pseudo-Areopagite made the basis for the Christian heaven of the Middle Ages. The number of angels varied in the works of different writers, and there was no consistent pattern in the hierarchy until almost the beginning of the Christian era, but the vast multitude of heavenly beings was indicated by most writers in the familiar phrase "ten thousand times ten thousand."

The angels were classified according to their function, and except in a few rare instances only the lowest ranks became messengers between heaven and earth. There was considerable resemblance between the angels who were charged with the care of the forces of nature and the nature gods of other religions. In one of the visions in the first Book of Enoch, the writer is shown the portals of the stars and sees how their motions are controlled, as well as the portals of the rain, wind, frost, and dew, each under the supervision of its particular angel.

The highest ranks of angels, those that had their abode in the upper heavens, were concerned only with heavenly matters, and each rank was headed by an angel prince.

Closest of all to the divine presence were the cherubim and seraphim. The so-called "cherub" of later Christian art, consisting of a detached childish head between a pair of wings, is far removed from the cherubim that appeared in the visions of Ezekiel. The "living creatures" he saw bore no resemblance to the "men" who appeared to Abraham and Jacob. To modern minds, unaccustomed to apocalyptic writing, they are likely to seem more bizarre than awe-inspiring. The description Ezekiel gave was wholly symbolic and was intended to express the ineffable by means of imagery that had meaning for his contemporaries. Three of the four faces of the cherubim, the bull, the lion, and the water-carrier, are found among the fixed signs of the zodiac, the origin of which is very ancient. The fourth, the eagle, since it is said to renew its youth, has been thought to be interchangeable with the phoenix, which in turn takes the place of the zodiacal scorpion, because both are associated with resurrection through fire. The Christian Fathers, looking back on Old Testament prophecy in the light of their faith, saw all such symbols as relating to Christ. Thus the four faces of the cherubim became emblems of the four Evangelists and found their way into the decorations of many early churches.

Their original meaning in human terms, forgotten through the familiarity of long use of the symbols themselves, has been expressed in different forms in more modern times. William Blake, whose visions were perhaps comparable to those of the Hebrew prophets, saw in "four Zoas" representations of man's imagination, reason, passion, and instincts, the four forming the complete human being. In the golden age of eternity, Blake said, man was a unity.

In his view, the fall of man consisted of the breaking up of the unity into parts, of which one became dominant. More than a century later, the psychologist Carl Gustav Jung, writing from a scientific point of view, described what he called "the four functions" of man as intuition, thinking, feeling, and sensation. Much of the psychic imbalance of Western men and women in our time he attributed to the loss from consciousness of one of the four functions. It would be carrying the interpretation too far to assign one of the faces of the cherub to each of these parts of the psyche, for the bull, the lion, and the eagle had many meanings in the ancient world, but the sense of a whole composed of four differentiated parts seems to have been as strong in Ezekiel's time as it was to the poet Blake or the scientist Jung.

Even more fantastic in our sight than the four faces and the two pairs of wings which clothed Ezekiel's "living creatures" are the wheels by means of which they moved. The wheel, as a circle, also expresses wholeness, and it is associated with motion, so that it is not surprising to find the wheels of the cherubim moving of their own accord. The rims of the wheels were full of eyes, for they were the guiding force for the cherubim, who must see where they were going. "Whithersoever the spirit was to go, they went; thither the spirit was to go. . . . for the spirit of the living creatures was in the wheels." The wheels moved the cherubim up and down and in any one of the four directions, but they could not turn them from a straight course. One is reminded of the "spirit walls" that screened the entrance doors to old Chinese courtyards. These were intended to keep out evil influences, since spirits could travel only in straight lines and therefore could not pass around them.

Ezekiel's symbolism has lost its emotional power in our day, but something of its grandeur was caught by another exiled people, the American Negroes.

> Ezekiel saw the wheel
> Way up in the middle of the air.
> Ezekiel saw the wheel
> Way in the middle of the air.
>
> And the big wheel runs by faith
> And the little wheel runs by the grace of God—
> A wheel in a wheel
> Way in the middle of the air.

It was "living creatures" such as these who guarded the gate of Paradise after Adam and Eve were expelled, but the sword of flame that "turned every way, to keep the way of the tree of life" may have been a separate phenomenon, for the story says God placed the cherubim *and* the flaming sword at the east gate. Fire played an important part in the picture of heaven. A perpetual stream of fire flowed from under the throne of God, and some of the rabbinic writings said that new angels were constantly being created out of this divine element, whose whole duty was to praise the Lord until they were dissolved again into the flame. Since human beings associate fire with the passions that stir them to the extremes of ecstasy and pain, the divine fire embodied in the chanting host is a concept that must have been deeply moving to the religious imagination. From the throne itself, described by Ezekiel, with careful avoidance of the literal, as "the *likeness* of a throne" from which there came "the *appearance* of fire," issued the eternal light, too strong, perhaps, even for the eyes of the seraphim. This is suggested by Isaiah, the only writer to describe this class of beings, when he explained that one of their three pairs of wings was to cover their faces. Effulgence surrounded and radiated from the angels themselves, so that when they were seen by men on earth they were described as wearing shining garments.

It was in the post-exile writings that the archangels first appeared and were given names. Many of the exiled Jews had been in Persia, where the religion of Zoroaster was a fresh and vital influence. There was no idolatry in Zoroastrianism, which recognized one supreme god, but there were six holy spirits emanating from him, who with him constituted the godhead. The six represented fundamental ethical and spiritual values. This idea may have been a source for the development in Jewish thought of the concept of a superior class of angels with individual characteristics and special functions within the celestial hierarchy.

The number of the archangels, and even some of their names, did not become fixed in the pre-Christian era. Some of the writers mention four, and others seven, and of those whose names remained constant there were only three: Michael, Gabriel, and Raphael. The fourth place was eventually taken by Uriel, whose name remained among both the Christians and the Moslems, but various other names appeared in the Jewish writings, such as Phanuel, Raguel, Saraquel, Remiel, the more obscure Sandalphon, whose name has to do with great height, and Ridya, who appears to be related to the world of nature in the form of rain.

The distinction between archangels and angel princes is also far from clear, though sometimes a name appears in both categories. Authorities differed also on the functions of Michael, Gabriel, Raphael, and Uriel, but Michael consistently took first place in the list and was counted in rabbinical literature as one of the angel princes, charged with the special care of the Hebrew nation. His pre-eminence was carried over into the Christian hierarchy, but in Jewish literature he yielded place to a still higher angel, Metatron, the throne angel, who was permitted to sit in the divine chamber to record the deeds of Israel. Metatron was identified with Enoch, who, according to the Book of Genesis, lived 365 years and walked with God. Since Enoch did not die, but "he was not, for God took him," his disappearance called for explanation, and he was accorded high honor in heaven.

Michael was taken over by the Christians as guardian of the Church and was considered the angel of judgment, who was to weigh the souls of the dead. Gabriel, on the other hand, who had held that position in the Jewish hierarchy, became among the Christians the archangel of heavenly mercy. Raphael, whose name means "God heals," remained the angel of providence, watching over men. Uriel appears less often in art and literature; his name means the glorious light that flows from the throne of God. As a bringer of light, he became the angel of interpretation, carrying a scroll as his symbol.

Michael was the only archangel to whom the Jews gave the guardianship of a particular nation, but each known nation, whether or not it recognized the god of the Hebrews, had one of the seventy angel princes assigned to it.

These princes also formed a court or heavenly council and are spoken of as rulers of the planets. Guardianship of individual human beings was put in the hands of innumerable angels of a lower order, though the archangels were said to have felt particular concern for the salvation of men. The "joy in heaven over one sinner that repenteth," would not be confined to the sinner's personal guardian, or even to those of his own rank, but would be felt by their superiors as well.

Many people have had the notion that the souls of the dead were believed to become angels on their entry into heaven, or that they took a form that enabled them to live intimately among the angels. The popular picture, often derisively drawn, of the soul dressed in white robes, sitting on a cloud and playing a harp, must have come from this idea. Actually, the spiritual world as seen in the literature of the rabbis allows for a separate dwelling place for the souls of the righteous.

In the center of the seventh heaven was the throne of God, and surrounding it, but separated from it by a curtain of cloud, so that those on the other side could hear God's voice but could not see him, was the circle of the souls of the righteous. They were nearer to the throne than were the angels, who were said to have to ask the human souls concerning the deeds of God. Indeed, the angels, while performing the work of God, were not thought to be omniscient, but only carried out the missions on which they were sent, and took the responsibilities assigned to them. They had the power to appear in any form appropriate to the occasion, so that sometimes their identity as celestial beings may be in doubt. Their functions were many, but it is uncertain whether the same angel might perform various tasks or each was given one task of a particular kind. The angel of death may not always be the same angel, but those that control the forces of nature seem to have been fixed in their positions. The personal guardian, also, remained the same throughout the lifetime of a human being, whether he was good or evil. The duty above all other duties for every angel was to sing praises, and music has been, in both Jewish and Christian times, an indispensable part of the order of the spiritual world.

Into this picture of eternal light and endless song, of awful majesty and perfect order, came ever more insistently the dark shadows of the evil which men experienced on earth. This burden of mankind had to be accounted for in some way, and as the Jews mingled with other nations they were exposed to many new ideas. The simple relationship between the people and their patriarchal god, whose deeds could not be questioned whether or not they seemed just, and whose everlasting laws were known, no longer held all the answers to problems encountered in a wider world. The rabbis made increasingly complicated interpretations of scripture, illustrated by stories drawn from ancient legends that sometimes fitted only loosely with the Biblical text. Sects arose making rival claims to the truth and setting enlightenment against orthodoxy. Most strongly felt among the foreign influences was Zoroastrianism, as we have already seen, for it held many parallels to the religion of the Jews. Although Jewish orthodoxy still recognized only a single principle under one omnipotent god, there was a strong appeal in the duality of the Zoroastrian belief in separate powers of good and evil. In the Talmud, the great collection of Jewish writings, can be seen the gradual development of a new doctrine of evil, which, if it did not represent the strictest views of the authorities, became widespread among the people.

Satan, as the personification of evil, became more and more the source of all that was opposed to the will of God. Nowhere in the books that make up the Hebrew Bible is there a reference to Satan as a power in his own right. He is mentioned only a few times, and only in documents written after the exile, but in each of these passages he still appears as a member of the court of heaven under God's command. His name, which means "the adversary," places him in a peculiar position—standing by the throne of God to challenge, to cast doubt on judgments, and to offer temptation to men, in order to prove the absolute righteousness and power of God. He seems to have been "the devil's advocate" before he became the devil himself. In many rabbinical writings he also appeared as the angel of death, since death has usually seemed to men evil. Gradually stories came into being that showed his transformation into an independent ruler of the kingdom of evil. The orthodox still did not identify him with the serpent that tempted Eve, but stories of his fall through jealousy of Adam and of the fall of man through Satan's guile became current and established themselves in the minds of the people, to whom myth spoke more strongly than precept.

Since heaven could not contain him any longer, Satan was said to have been expelled from its sacred precincts and to have gathered to himself the forces of evil, consisting both of his followers among the angels who were expelled with him and of the many demons who inhabited the upper air and moved freely about the earth. These demons, whose existence was generally accepted throughout the ancient world, had become very real to the Jews and now played an important part in their lives, since most of the ills and errors of mankind were attributed to them. With Satan, or a similar figure under another name, as their leader, a whole mythology developed which was used retrospectively to explain evil events of the past as revealed in the scriptures. Speculation as to the time and circumstances of Satan's creation, the reasons that led to his expulsion from heaven, and the future judgment and punishment he was to undergo took various forms. In no case, however, was he thought of as separated from the universe created by Yahweh, but rather as one of the sons of God who had rebelled and been cast out.

Since angels had hitherto represented attributes of God and were incapable of action other than to carry out God's will, it became necessary to reconsider their nature. Much was made of the statement in Genesis 6:2 that "the sons of God saw the daughters of men that they were fair; and they took them wives of all that they chose." The meaning of the phrase "the sons of God" was open to dispute and was given several interpretations. The one most acceptable to later Jewish orthodoxy intimates that the misalliance occurred between "the sons of the mighty ones" among the human race and the inferior women who happened to attract them; but meanwhile popular imagination had accepted the giants and the demons as the result of unholy unions between angels and the daughters of men. Even though the wickedness of man that led to the flood was a consequence of these events, the fallen angels were credited with having taught the people of earth the skills and arts of civilization. This idea lingered on into medieval Christianity, when Satan was considered to be in such complete control of the material world that some persons saw him as its creator. Life became a continuous struggle against the forces of evil in many bodily forms. Since the demons inhabited the lower heavens—as the Greeks also believed—at any moment one of them might appear in a visible form of his own choice, to tempt, torment, or bring sickness or even death to individual human beings.

The religious community that produced the Dead Sea Scrolls found at Qumran subscribed fully to the theory of the kingdom of Satan. Founded about 200 B.C. and continuing until the destruction of the Temple at Jerusalem by Titus, the community of the followers of the Teacher of Righteousness was well established and actively concerned with the spiritual life of its people during the lifetime of Jesus of Nazareth, though no one knows how far its influence spread. To these people, the forces of good and evil were both created by one sovereign god, who decreed that some men should be ruled by one and some by the other. During their own era the two forces were to have equal power, but they looked forward to the time when a great conflict between the two would occur. As representatives of "the Sons of Light," these men were dedicated to preparing for the appointed day when the Archangel Michael would lead his hosts to victory over "the Sons of Darkness." They thought of themselves as "the remnant" or "the survivors of the Covenant," who were to be organized under special groups of angels to meet the challenge from the armies of evil. Satan's name appears many times in their

Satan

hymns. He was both the enemy of God and the means by which God would punish those who had pursued the evil path. A passage in the scrolls that comprises the War Rule declares: "But Satan, the Angel of Malevolence, Thou hast created for the Pit; his [rule] is in Darkness and his purpose is to bring about wickedness and iniquity." Before his power is destroyed and he is consigned to the pit for eternity, however, Satan will be let loose on the earth.

> The torrents of Satan shall reach
> to all sides of the world. . . .
> And all those upon it shall rave
> and shall perish amid the great misfortune.
> For God shall sound His mighty voice
> and His holy abode shall thunder
> with the truth of His glory.
> The heavenly hosts shall cry out
> and the world's foundations
> shall stagger and sway.
> The war of the heavenly warriors shall scourge the earth;
> and it shall not end before the appointed destruction
> which shall be for ever and without compare.[1]

After the destruction of the world comes fulfillment in heaven for the righteous. Among the fragments of liturgical writings found at Qumran is a hymn concerning the blessings of the seven princes of heaven on all the companions of righteousness, and a prose passage describes the glory of their abode. The picture is derived from the visions of Ezekiel, but the wheels that in his text were said to accompany the cherubim had been fastened by succeeding generations to the throne of sapphire, perhaps through sheer inability to conceive of living wheels that acted independently. Drawn by the cherubim themselves, instead of moving them, this throne-chariot remained a subject for meditation in later Jewish mysticism and persisted in Christian iconography not only to the time of Dante but much later to the imagery of William Blake.[2] To members of the Essene community at Qumran the throne-chariot of God was a focal point for worship, as they added their praises to those of the angelic host. It is noteworthy that in the following passage from their ritual, full of motion, color, and the sound of praise, it is the "still small voice" first heard by Elijah that brings the blessing.

> The Cherubim bless the image of the Throne-Chariot above the firmament, and they praise the [majesty] of the fiery firmament beneath the seat of His glory. And between the turning wheels, Angels of Holiness come and go, as it were a fiery vision of most holy spirits; and about them [flow] seeming rivulets of fire, like gleaming bronze, a radiance of many gorgeous colors, of marvelous pigments magnificently mingled.
>
> The spirits of the Living God move perpetually with the glory of the wonderful chariot. The small voice of blessing accompanies the tumult as they depart, and on the path of their return they worship the Holy One. Ascending, they rise marvelously; settling, they [stay] still. The sound of joyful praise is silenced and there is a small voice of blessing in all the camp of God. And a voice of praise [resounds] from the midst of all their divisions in [worship] . . . and each one in his place, all their numbered ones sing hymns of praise.

Such were the current views of the spiritual world as the Christian era began. Except for certain sects or groups who followed a particular teaching, there never was a completely consistent pattern in the accepted concepts of the Jews. The borderline between doctrine and folklore is indistinct, and the popular beliefs of the time are often reflected in the writings of the New Testament. Within broad outlines, however, there was no break in the traditions, and Jewish concepts formed the background for the Christian beliefs concerning heaven and the angels.

3 / INTERLUDE

A tale should be judicious, clear, succinct;
The language plain, the incidents well linked;
Tell not as new what ev'rybody knows,
And, new or old, still hasten to a close.
—WILLIAM COWPER

Two of the most widely known and best-loved stories of angels' intervention were written at a time in Jewish history when the religious authorities had relegated the angels to an increasingly inaccessible and elaborate heaven. If the people failed to find heavenly messengers at work on the earth in their own time, they still saw events in the past that indicated their immediate presence in the affairs of man. Such stories as those concerning Daniel and Tobias must have made a strong appeal to their desire for supernatural aid, quite aside from such pious attitudes as the books were designed to promote.

It is agreed by most modern scholars that the narrative of the Book of Daniel has little historical foundation; the collection of stories it contains may have been derived from legendary material. A man named Daniel is mentioned in the Book of Ezekiel, linked with Noah and Job, as one of the supremely righteous men of the past. Placed among the prophets in the Christian canon of the Old Testament, the Book of Daniel is said to have been written in the time of the Maccabees, during the second century before Christ, to encourage the hopes of the Jews in a troubled period by recalling the faith of their forefathers in the years of exile in Babylon. The story of Tobias and the archangel Raphael, told in the Book of Tobit, was written at about the same time and is placed in a still earlier setting at Nineveh, following an invasion of Palestine by the Assyrians. Both stories concern displaced persons, as we should call them today, and the situations they describe resemble conditions experienced by minority groups in many times and places.

Even if the Book of Daniel, containing both narrative and prophecy, was put together by one man, the story itself could hardly be called the work of one man's imagination, for it follows a popular pattern. Like Joseph, Daniel was a captive in a foreign land who won a high position at court through his ability to interpret dreams, but his adventures were more colorful than Joseph's, since the latter's good fortune remained with him throughout his life. The incident that has given him his greatest fame is his rescue from appalling danger, to which his faithfulness to his God had subjected him. His being thrown to the lions and coming out unscathed seems to be the most memorable event in the tale, perhaps because the terror of wild beasts is a particularly primitive form of fear to which everyone can respond. The adventure of Daniel's three friends, which precedes the episode of the lions in the narrative, actually presents a greater miracle, since the action of fire is even more predictable than the ferocity of beasts.

The three youths, who with Daniel had been chosen from among the captive Jews to be attendants on King Nebuchadnezzar and to be educated in the palace, are usually known by their Babylonian names, Shadrach, Meshach, and Abednego. All four remained true to their religion, but while Daniel still remained in favor, the other three were charged with disloyalty when they refused to worship the gods of their master, and were cast into a furnace so hot that the men who threw them in were themselves consumed by the fire. When Nebuchadnezzar sent for a report on the death of the young men, he was astonished to hear that there were four men walking in the midst of the flames and that the fourth was like a son of the gods. Struck with awe, the king was convinced that the god of the victims had sent his angel to their aid, and they were immediately restored to their trusted positions.

Daniel's own position at the Babylonian court remained secure through the reigns of Nebuchadnezzar and his son Belshazzar, and it was not until Babylon was conquered by the Persians that he was put through his ordeal. By this time he must have been an old man and he had reached such importance that the conquerors appointed him one of three governors under whom the country was ruled. It was a plot of the jealous Persian satraps under him that brought on him the test of his faith. When these men contrived a law which they persuaded the king to sign, forbidding the people to make any petition except to him, Daniel deliberately let himself be seen praying to God by his window, which stood open toward Jerusalem. Appalled by the consequences of having put his name to a law which could not be revoked, because "the law of the Medes and the Persians altereth not," the king, whose power proved to be weaker than his word, spent the night in sleepless fasting while his trusted aide was sealed in the den of the lions, and in the morning went himself to find out what had occurred. It was with great relief and gladness that he heard Daniel's words, "My God hath sent his angel and hath shut the lions' mouths, and they have not hurt me." The retribution that the king exacted in the destruction not only of the perfidious satraps but of their entire families was characteristic of the times of well as of the vindictive mood commonly found in folk tales of all times.

The angels in the story of Daniel differ from those in the earlier books of the Bible in that they are sent to the rescue of the hero as a reward for his faith rather than to bring him a new spiritual experience such as occurred in some form in each of the angel episodes in Genesis. Such miraculous happenings were to be narrated countless times in the Christian era in the legends of the saints. The function of rescuer, however, was not the only one performed by angels in the Book of Daniel, for they appear in their early role of messengers in the chapters containing the prophecies which the writer attributes to the hero of his narrative, and in which he delivers his message to the people of his own time.

Daniel's visions, as set down here, are said to have been interpreted for him by an angelic visitant. Writing in the first person, he says, "Yea, while I was speaking in prayer, the man Gabriel, whom I had seen in the vision at the beginning, being caused to fly swiftly, touched me about the time of the evening oblation. And he instructed me and talked with me, and said, O Daniel, I am now come forth to give thee wisdom and understanding. At the beginning of thy supplications the commandment went forth, and I am come to tell thee; for thou art greatly beloved, therefore consider the matter and understand the vision." This is the only appearance of one of the archangels in any of the books that now make up the Protestant Old Testament. The word "man" associated with the name Gabriel gives the impression that the concept of the archangel was still indeterminate. Perhaps he had not yet permanently assumed wings, for the text says he had been "caused to fly swiftly," as if he had been given wings for this particular errand. In the somewhat later Book of Noah, containing some of the visions of Enoch, the angels were said to have taken to themselves wings in order to carry out special missions. In any case, Gabriel appeared before Daniel as a man, and this time, to make it clear that it was no vision but reality, Daniel said that Gabriel touched him. There were other appearances, such as "one whose body was like beryl and his face like lightning," but again the angel who came to comfort him appeared as a man. In the revelations that followed concerning the final deliverance of the Hebrews, Daniel prophesied that leadership would come from Michael, "the great prince who standeth for thy people." His hopes were similar to those expressed in the Qumran scrolls, and echoes of the same idea were to be heard many times in the succeeding centuries.

The Book of Tobit does not claim to be anything but fiction, even though, like Daniel, it was written with the purpose of instilling faith and courage in the minds of people whose religious life was threatened by political oppression. It was never a part of the Jewish canon of scripture and it is no longer included in the Protestant Bible, but when the world contained no printed books and the old tales were read over and over, Tobias and his traveling companion were among the favorite figures of romance for countless generations. Students of art are familiar with the many representations by medieval and Renaissance painters of the youthful Tobias accompanied by his pet dog and conducted on his journey by the archangel Raphael. Where he was going and why are not so well remembered. It is a pity that the artists for the most part neglected the other scenes in the story, which are rich in human interest, for the book contains distinct and varied characters in action that follows the themes of misfortune and success, of innocence and guile, and of the power of love and kindness. Conforming to the accustomed ways of portraying angels, the painters usually showed Raphael, whose assistance is central to the plot, in full heavenly regalia instead of in the disguise in which Tobias saw him as a human traveler.

The story begins and ends at Nineveh, the capital of Assyria, where the Jews were persecuted during the reign of Sennacherib. Tobit, a Jew of the dispersion, had become wealthy in the service of Sennacherib's father, Sargon, here called Enemessar. He had banked part of his wealth with a relative who lived near Ecbatana in Media. Because Tobit had been faithful to his religion during the persecution and had sought out and buried the bodies of the slain Jews, all that he had left had been taken from him. He was old and blind, and his wife, Anna, had been obliged to take in sewing to support the family. In despair Tobit wished that he might die and prayed to God to take him, but, giving thought to the future of his son Tobias, he prepared to send him to claim the funds that had been entrusted to the distant relative, urging him also, as Isaac urged Jacob, to bring back a wife from among his own kinsmen.

At the very time that the old man was praying for death at Nineveh, a young Jewish woman in Media was also praying in great distress that she might die, for she had been accused by her maids of having strangled seven men to whom she had been successively married and who had died mysteriously on the wedding night in each instance.

Tobit's prayer was answered, not by the angel of death but by the archangel Raphael, the healer, who embodied the divine providence watching over men. Raphael appeared as a man calling himself Azarias, who proposed to act as guide to the young Tobias, and the two set out for the long journey to Media, attended by the only dog memorialized in the scriptures as a companion to man. The Vulgate version of the book records the wagging of the dog's tail at the time of the successful return from the quest.

The element of magic soon enters the story and takes an important part in the action. When the travelers reached the banks of the Tigris a huge fish leaped out of the river and was caught by Tobias, who at the direction of his guide cut it open and preserved the heart, liver, and gall for later use against evil spirits. It was the foreknowledge of the angel that caused him to take this precaution, for the innocent youth and the maiden in distress were soon to meet. Raphael knew that the Persian demon Asmodeus had

[47

been haunting the girl and that it was he who in jealousy had slain the seven bridegrooms. Sara, the daughter of Raguel and Edna, was of course destined to become the bride of Tobias, not without some trepidation on both sides. When the marriage contract had been signed, Raphael was able to allay the fears of the bridegroom and give him instructions before the two young people were left together. Tobias burned the heart and liver of the fish in the bridal chamber, and the smoke drove the demon away as far as upper Egypt, where, the text says, "the angel bound him." It is understandable that in the spiritual world physical distance is of no account, but it is noteworthy that in the writer's mind even angelic power was not able to destroy the demon—only to banish him.

While the wedding was being celebrated, Raphael's next act of kindness was to complete the journey alone and collect the money which was the object of the expedition. After fourteen days the young people set out with their guide and the dog and returned to Nineveh, where the aged parents were waiting in acute anxiety on account of the delay in their son's arrival. Leaving Sara by the gate of the city, the two men went ahead to prepare the old couple for her coming. After a joyful reception, Tobias's first act was to use the gall of the fish to cure his father's blindness, whereupon the old man went out to welcome his daughter-in-law at the entrance to the city.

It was not until seven days of celebration had been completed that Tobit, with his son's ready assent, generously offered the man Azarias half of the money he had brought from Media. In replying to the offer Azarias said, "It is good to keep close the secret of a king, but it is honorable to reveal the works of God." Then he told them that he was Raphael, "one of the seven holy angels, which present the prayers of the saints, and which go in and out before the glory of the Holy One." While the amazed family prostrated themselves before the angel he disappeared and was seen no more. After the hymn of praise and thanksgiving that closes the episode, the author, loyal to his characters to the end, carries them through the years to the death of Tobias at the age of 127. On the advice of his father, who had foreseen the destruction of Nineveh, he had moved to Ecbatana, where he lived out his days in wealth and happiness, surrounded by many descendants. A simple piety sheds a soft glow over the whole tale, in which goodness is rewarded, evil is punished, love is consummated, the poor become rich, and the miraculous is the close accompaniment of the earthly. If the story satisfies the appetite for marvels—to use a phrase of Andrew Lang's—and if the archangel whom the author employs as *deus ex machina* appears completely at home in his human form, he suffers no such loss of dignity as he would if he were seen as a magician, but is felt throughout to be the true representative of the guiding power of God in the affairs of men.

4 / THE NEW DISPENSATION

While shepherds watched their flocks by night,
All seated on the ground,
The angel of the Lord came down,
And glory shone around.

— NAHUM TATE

When the followers of Jesus began to record in writing their new experience of God-in-man and the books now a part of the New Testament and others not in the canon were written, much of the Jewish tradition was carried over into the new doctrine. It would be impossible for the average reader to distinguish between the Jewish heaven and that of the early Christians except for the presence there of the risen Christ. But the new religious force was so real to those who were converts that they saw with fresh eyes and greater simplicity the relations between God and man. While their concept of the spiritual world with its heavenly court and its ranks of angels remained essentially the same, there was evident in their writing a return to the idea of direct revelation from God through angelic messengers. There is an intimacy in the encounters with angels recorded in the Gospels that recalls the simplicity and the closeness to human life of the stories in Genesis. This was a new beginning.

Zachariah the old priest, burning incense in the temple, saw an angel standing close to him on the right side of the altar. The definiteness with which the angel is placed at the right, not the left, adds reality to the scene and gives an impression of authority, as when the Old Testament writers speak of "the right hand of God." Zachariah was struck dumb by the vision and could only make signs to the people waiting outside, but later the presence of the angel was as vividly recalled as his message foretelling the birth to the old man and his wife Elizabeth of a son who was to become John the Baptist.

When the archangel Gabriel appeared to Elizabeth's cousin Mary, the betrothed of Joseph the carpenter of Nazareth, she not only saw him and heard him but carried on a conversation with him. The scene as it is given to us by the many painters who have portrayed it usually shows Mary already glorified as she was in the minds of the devout in the artist's own time. She is seen in a setting of richness and dignity worthy of the Holy Mother she was to become, even though her posture of humility and awe may be deeply felt. The Gospel story, however, is a simple account of the remarkable experience of a girl at home in a hill town of Galilee, questioning the meaning of the angel's salutation and accepting, even though it was beyond her understanding, the role that was laid upon her by God. In the interview, Gabriel entered the women's world so completely that the means he used to bring home to Mary the reality of divine intervention was the announcement of Elizabeth's miraculous pregnancy in her old age. Mary would need sympathetic companionship in her new experience, and Gabriel wisely brought the two women together. It was through contact with another human being who had felt the power of God that assurance came to Mary, finding expression in a poem which the writer puts into her mouth.

For such a delicate mission Gabriel, whose name means "the hero of God," seems at first a strange choice. The Hebrew writers represented him as the angel of judgment carrying a sword, and it was he who was said to have destroyed Sodom and who struck the servants of the Egyptian princess who tried to prevent her from drawing Moses out of the bulrushes. Michael was said to be made of snow, but Gabriel was made of fire. Fire was, after all, a symbol of the Holy Spirit, which he promised would come upon Mary under the shadow of the power of God. The lilies which medieval painters placed in Gabriel's hand were a token of the purity of the Virgin whom he was seen to adore rather than a symbol of the creative Spirit for whom he was the harbinger.

It was Luke who told the story of the annunciation, but Matthew recorded Joseph's doubts about his coming marriage when he learned that Mary was already with child. The angel whose words brought relief from his anxiety appeared to him not in a waking vision but in a dream. Some dreams speak to the dreamer with as much authority as if he had experienced them awake, and Joseph's dream is described as of such power and vividness that the authenticity of the angel's message was never in doubt.

On the night of Jesus' birth, the story says, the shepherds in the fields outside Bethlehem saw an angel standing with them on the ground. We are apt to forget this in telling the story, for the quiet presence is overlooked in the light of "the glory of the Lord" which "shone round about them." In contrast to the King James version, which says the angel "came upon them," the New English Bible translation brings him down to earth by saying, "Suddenly there stood before them an angel of the Lord." Suddenly and directly confronted, it is no wonder that the humble shepherds were terror-struck and needed the assurance of the angel that he brought them good news. It was not until he had given them the utterly human and practical details of how to find the babe in the manger that the heavenly host began its song of praise.

The next appearance of angels in the Gospel record is much less definite. They are only alluded to in the story of the temptation of Jesus, while the figure of Satan stands out with clarity, as it usually does in reports of encounters with him. All three of the synoptic Gospels give the story of the forty days in the wilderness when Jesus withdrew from the crowds that had witnessed his baptism by John. What actually happened there can only be conjectural, for so far as we know, no one went with him. According to the fourth Gospel, it was while he was with John by the Jordan that Jesus found Andrew and Peter, who became his first disciples, though the others set the scene of their calling beside the Sea of Galilee. If Jesus, returning to Galilee from his ordeal in the wilderness, spoke of it to Peter, the latter probably told the story to Mark, who is understood to have heard the events of Jesus' life from him; yet Mark's account is a starkly brief outline. As it appears in the King James version, the passage reads:

> And immediately the Spirit driveth him forth into the wilderness. And he was there in the wilderness forty days, tempted of Satan; and he was with the wild beasts; and the angels ministered unto him.

Satan, the wild beasts, and the angels are all included in the scene, but how they may have played their parts is left entirely to the imagination. In Matthew's version, the wild beasts are omitted, but the ministration of the angels is connected with the departure of the devil; he mentions neither the beasts nor the angels. John omits the whole episode.

It was characteristic of Jesus to withdraw from society at crucial times, when he needed solitude to commune with God. There was plenty of precedent in the Hebrew scriptures for the forty days' fast, since both Moses and Elijah had spent similar periods in fasting. The time of testing and preparation could be taken as a sign of the authenticity of Jesus' mission. Satan is seen here in his Old Testament role. What sets Mark's account apart from the others is the inclusion of the animals. He does not suggest that Jesus was in danger from them, though that idea could be implicit in his statement. It is also possible to infer that they were his companions. The animals and the angels, as Mark wrote of them, seem to have equal places in the events, as if together they represented a whole made up of earth and heaven.

The poet Robert Graves, impressed by this aspect of the story, wrote a poem called "In the Wilderness," in which he pictures as Jesus' companion the scapegoat that had been accursed and turned loose in the desert.

Then ever with him went,
Of all his wanderings
Comrade, with ragged coat,
Gaunt ribs—poor innocent—
Bleeding feet, burning throat,
The guileless young scapegoat;
For forty nights and days
Followed in Jesus' ways
Sure guard behind him kept,
Tears like a lover wept.[1]

To the poet, the scapegoat, which also bore the guilt of the people, acted the part of the guardian angel. He was not the first to think of the connection, for Barnabas, speaking of the scapegoat, said in his General Epistle, "Consider how exactly this appears to have been a type of Jesus." Barnabas was writing not poetry but an exposition of Hebrew scriptures from a Christian viewpoint. Mark, however, in his simple statements left the way open for the devoted and poetic imagination to fill in the functions of the beasts and the angels in the inner drama that took place in the days Jesus spent in solitude.

In the accounts of the three years of Jesus' ministry, there are no visitations by angels recorded, although Jesus mentioned angels often. Satan, as the author of evil and the tempter of men, appears as a living force in Jesus' teaching, and as prince of the demons that often caused human suffering. Possession by demons was a familiar phenomenon among the people who flocked to hear Jesus' message, and the form of exorcism he used was followed in the early Church, for demonology has had a long and active history. The Evil One was obviously of the earth, but the references to the angels in the teaching and preaching of Jesus are chiefly to their functions in the spiritual world. The armies of God still existed, for him, in heaven.

One of the statements about angels attributed to Jesus seems to depart from the accepted views. Using little children as models of simplicity and humility, Jesus made, according to the Matthew narrative, a surprising remark about the guardian angels of these little ones. He placed the attendant spirits of the children not in the lowest rank of angels, as befitted the worldly position of those whom they guarded, but so close to God himself that they could always see his face. The Jewish tradition had made heaven's central presence inaccessible. Even the souls of the righteous dead were removed and screened from the throne room, and, aside from the cherubim and seraphim, the angel of the throne himself was the only one who was allowed to remain in the divine chamber. Jesus' heretical teaching not only elevated children to a position of special consideration on earth, but opened doors in heaven itself. The Church Fathers never adopted the throne angel, Metatron, but their conception of the heavenly hierarchy seems to have been hardly less elastic than that of the rabbis. The intrusion of the personal guardians of the little children was apparently overlooked, even when the Holy Child himself began to be worshiped.

Except for a reference in the Gospel of Luke to the appearance of an angel to Jesus during the agony in the garden of Gethsemane, angels do not again appear in the Gospel story until after his death. They are seen then with the same intimacy with which they appear in the scenes of the Nativity. The story of the first Easter is told in all four

Gospels, but the accounts vary in detail. Matthew and Mark report that the first visitors to the tomb were the two Marys. Matthew introduces an earthquake, which occurs when the angel descends from heaven. It is clear that the writer uses the earthquake not to explain the open tomb but to emphasize the power of God, since he explicitly states that the angel came and rolled away the stone from the entrance. As if to prove that he had done so, the angel then sat down upon it. He was there not to arouse fear or awe but to console two human beings who had loved the crucified one, and sitting down brings ease into any situation where doubt or fear exists.

Mark's angel was also sitting down, but was discovered inside the tomb, on the right side. Luke gives the names of three women who were present, and he adds a second angel. In his account the angels appeared beside the women. They looked like men—there was no mention of the wings that painters later gave them—but they wore shining garments. John's version tells that Mary Magdalene alone was the first to visit the tomb, and at first she saw no one. When she saw the stone taken away she ran in fear to fetch Peter, who came with another disciple. The two men looked into the empty tomb while Mary stood outside, weeping. When the two men left she stayed behind, and it was then she looked into the tomb and saw two angels in white, sitting at the head and foot of the place where the body had lain. It was after they had asked her why she was weeping that she turned and saw Jesus himself, whom she at first took to be the gardener.

From the inconsistency of these accounts of the empty tomb it is obvious that there was no version that was generally accepted as authentic. The story must have spread rapidly among the scattered groups of early believers, taking new shapes as it went. Since the disciples had declared they had seen the risen Christ, the question must naturally have been "How did it happen?" Out of what he had heard, each writer seems to have chosen what was meaningful to him, and he doubtless gave it a form of his own. Wherever the laws of nature seemed to have been broken, angels played a part in the event as God's agents.

After the apostles had met the risen Jesus, we are told in the first chapter of Acts, they stood gazing intently into the sky, where he had disappeared. Suddenly "two men in white apparel" appeared beside them where they stood, asked them why they were standing there looking after him, and reassured them that they would see him come again as they saw him go. Since the Acts of the Apostles is a continuation of the Gospel of Luke, it is interesting to note that again there are two angels in this incident as there were in the story of the empty tomb. In both stories there are doubt and uncertainty about the fact and the meaning of the resurrection, and perhaps the doubling of messengers serves to enhance the majesty of the Lord and the force of his message.

In later angelic appearances in Acts, there is one angel only. When Peter and John were thrown into prison in Jerusalem, it was a single angel who opened the door and released them. The centurion Cornelius, who was to be the first follower among the gentiles, was visited by "a man in bright apparel" who told him to send for Peter. Paul, on the way to Rome as a prisoner, on a ship that was buffeted and helpless in a storm, was visited by an angel who "stood by" him and told him no lives would be lost.

Since the Holy Spirit had now come upon the apostles, an inner voice which is variously identified in different passages, even by the same writer, began to direct them. "The angel of the Lord" who spoke to Philip is referred to later in the same paragraph as "the Spirit." Ananias, who was sent to baptize Paul, heard "the voice of the Lord." When Peter was thinking over the vision that had come to him to prepare his mind for the acceptance of gentile converts, "the Spirit" directed him. When Paul and Silas were traveling together, they were forbidden first by "the Holy Spirit," then by "the Spirit of Jesus" to stop at certain places. The guiding voice, by whatever name it was called, was to them a real and powerful force. Whether it was associated with the earlier concept of "the angel of the Lord" or with the personality of the living Christ, or whether a wholly new emanation was thought to have come forth from God, the effect was of something that was given, not simply perceived, which seemed to have come from a source beyond the range of the human mind. "The angel," says Jung, "personifies the coming into consciousness of something new arising from the deep unconscious." [2] In the consciousness of these first Christians a new religion was being born.

5 / THE MARTYR'S CROWN

They climbed the steep ascent of heaven
Through peril, toil and pain.
—REGINALD HEBER

An immense outpouring of spiritual energy and passion marked the beginnings of the early Christian Church. The zeal of those for whom life had taken on a new meaning became a driving force in the communities of believers, and every aspect of the Christian way as to faith, morals, and observances was ardently discussed. At first the new world of the Christians centered in the expectation of the return of Christ within their own lifetime to take up his reign over the kingdom of which the state of redemption they now experienced made them already members. Their work was the regeneration of mankind, and the time was short, but those who charted the course found many causes for disagreement on questions of doctrine. Despite the emergence of factions and heresies, persecutions held them together.

Since Jewish concepts still formed the background from which the new religion had grown, the Jewish view of the spiritual world was little changed, although Greek elements appeared in the writings of the early Fathers, especially at Alexandria, where the philosophy of Philo had already brought Platonic forms of thinking into the Jewish doctrine. Speculation about the nature and functions of angels, however, did not play a large part in the thought of the Church during the first century, when living the Christian life in the midst of an antagonistic society demanded such endurance as only fully committed souls could muster. Angelic aid might be sought and sometimes found, but there was little incentive to seek new interpretations of experience in so strenuous a life. When Paul wrote to the Romans, "Who shall separate us from the love of Christ? shall tribulation, or anguish, or persecution, or famine, or nakedness, or peril, or sword?" he was speaking of the common lot of those to whom he wrote.

It was when the newness began to fade and the apostles and their followers had died without having seen the second coming of their Lord that thinking began to take new directions. Since Christ had not yet appeared on earth, the spiritual world in which he lived became again a matter for earnest exploration. Justin Martyr, writing at about the middle of the second century, assigned ethereal bodies to the angels and believed that they were fed by manna such as God gave the Israelites in the wilderness. From heaven they took care of all human beings. Demons tried to prevent men from conversion, and Justin looked upon heretics as tools of demons. The latter, however, could be exorcised "in the name of Jesus Christ, crucified under Pontius Pilate, governor of Judea." God had given Jesus such power that even the demons were overcome by hearing his name.

The apocryphal Apocalypse of Paul tells in detail about the activities of the guardian angels.

> When, therefore the sun is set, at the first hour of night, in the same hour goeth the angel of every people and of every man and woman, which protect and keep them, because man is the image of God: and likewise at the hour of morning which is the twelfth hour of the night, do all the angels of men and women go to meet God and present all the work, which every man has wrought, whether good or evil.

Bringing the figures of Greek mythology into his Christian eschatology, this writer said that the archangel Michael was the Psychopompus, who conducted the souls of the righteous to Paradise, as Tartarus conducted those who had done evil down to hell. It is evident that to the writer Paradise was a definite place, not a state of being, and that it was not situated in any of the heavens where the angels lived. Several writers of that time identified it with the Garden of Eden, vaguely placed somewhere "in the east," which man had lost through the fall of Adam and Eve. Through the redemptive power of Christ man could now regain his original home.

Clement of Alexandria compared the grades of bishops, priests, and deacons in the Church as it was already organized to the hierarchical order of angels in heaven. The Church was an imitation of the economy of the heavenly court, but the spiritual beings who inhabited heaven differed completely from the human members of its earthly counterpart. Since the angels carried men's prayers to God, they must understand men's thoughts, and since they had no senses with which to perceive, they must have instantaneous knowledge.

In the beginning of the third century, Origen, also a citizen of Alexandria, drew heavily from the concepts of Plato and Philo. To him angels were pure intelligences without any material form, yet he held to the Jewish doctrine concerning their fall from heaven. In his view, however, the fall of the angels was not due to their jealousy of man, as some had stated; reversing the sequence of events, he claimed that the creation of man came about as a result of the fall of the angels. Since man consisted of both body and soul, he was given the opportunity to struggle and to conquer sin. He could be helped in the battle by the angels in heaven and could be hindered by the demons, who existed because angels had fallen, but he retained his free will.

To the Christians of that time, life was indeed a continuous battle. They had to contend not only with human enemies but with the devil and all his hosts who inhabited the upper air and could take on material form at will. The old gods were now a part of this dark horde, for they could not at once pass into utter oblivion and when they were renounced they had to be reckoned with. The unconverted masses surrounding the Christian communities were still worshiping at their shrines and challenging the Christians to do likewise. The forces of darkness were often much more real to the followers of Jesus than the forces of light. Questions regarding the nature and functions of angels must have seemed of less importance to them than the hope that they might receive angelic aid in a world where torture was likely to be the reward of faithfulness. The message to the church at Smyrna in the Book of Revelation, "Be thou faithful unto death and I will give thee the crown of life," seems to have become not only a comforting promise but the expression of an ideal. So great was the desire for martyrdom in the time of Trajan that Ignatius of Antioch, arriving bound at Rome to be thrown to the wild beasts in the arena, felt it necessary to exhort his fellow Christians not to envy him as he hastened to his Lord.

The mark of the martyrs was joy. To die the same death as their Lord had suffered was to them the height of privilege—an attitude that doubtless added to the rage of their persecutors. Their delight in being chosen as worthy to become a sacrifice was enhanced by the belief that grew up concerning their admission to heaven. Among the writings of the time there are several suggestions that the souls of the righteous take on angelic form. In a letter from the church at Smyrna to the church at Philomelion, written about 156 A.D. by a certain Marcion, the martyrdom of Polycarp is described in detail. In praise of all the martyrs who had fallen in the persecution, the writer said: "And the fire of their inhuman torturers was cold to them, for their eyes were set on escape from the eternal fire which is never quenched, and with the eyes of the heart they looked upon the good things reserved for them that endure, which ear hath not heard nor eye seen, 'neither have they entered into the heart of man,' but they were revealed by the Lord unto them who were no longer men, but already angels."

It is possible that this writer was voicing a popular view rather than that of the great authorities. Tertullian, writing in the early years of the third century, said, "No one, on being absent from the body, is at once a dweller in the

presence of the Lord, except by the prerogative of martyrdom he gains a lodging in Paradise, not in the lower re-
gions." He makes it clear, however, that immediate entry
into Paradise does not mean becoming an angel. Writing
about the Last Judgment, which was to follow the
thousand-year reign of Christ on earth, he places the transformation of the soul far in the future. After the destruction
of the world by fire, he said, "We shall all be changed in a
moment into the substance of angels, even by the investi-
ture of an incorruptible nature, and so be removed to that
kingdom of heaven." This, of course, follows the teaching
of Paul, as given in the First Epistle to the Corinthians:
"For the trumpet shall sound, and the dead shall be raised
incorruptible."

Beginning with the terror directed against the Christians
under Nero at the time of the great fire at Rome, A.D. 64,
waves of persecution swept across the whole Mediterranean
world at intervals of forty or fifty years. Christianity was
made illegal in the time of Trajan, and while there were
periods of calm in which the Church grew despite its position, it was an uneasy peace, since certain local governors
were particularly assiduous in carrying out the law. The
last widespread persecution, under Diocletian, not only
took many lives but destroyed churches and books and
records. It may be for this reason that there are so few
eyewitness accounts in existence of the deaths of the martyrs. In view of the elaborate legends that were later told
about these early saints, the few contemporary accounts
that are available show a surprising simplicity.

The official records, such as those relating to the trials of
Justin, Cyprian, and the Martyrs of Scilli, tell only what

questions were asked and how they were answered, and of the sentences imposed. The narratives written by Christian eyewitnesses to inform their fellow believers go into greater detail and are concerned with inspiring in others the faith and courage displayed by those who had died. Few events that could be considered miraculous appear in these accounts, though two of them show how the spiritual exaltation that came upon the Christians who dared to be present colored their view of what they saw and heard.

In the same letter in which Marcion spoke of the victims as having already become angels, he tells that when the aged Polycarp entered the stadium a voice was heard from heaven saying, "Be strong, Polycarp, and play the man." After repeated refusals to abjure his Christian faith, he was bound to the stake and the fire was set. As it kindled, Marcion said, the fire rose around him in an arc like a bellying sail, forming a wall that did not touch his body. Since the fire refused to burn the martyr, the soldiers were ordered to thrust a dagger into his body. As he died, the brethren saw a dove rise up, and there was such a gush of blood that the fire was put out.

Eusebius the historian, writing at Caesarea more than a century later, described the trials and deaths of the martyrs of Palestine in his own time. Only one event that he recorded seemed to him miraculous. It occurred after the martyrdom of a young man named Epiphanius, who after repeated tortures was thrown into the sea. A great storm immediately arose, so that all the people trembled, and a tidal wave swept the body of the drowned man up onto the land and deposited it before the gate of the city. No one saw angels on these occasions, but the impression that some form of divine intervention had occurred took hold of the minds of those who had been deeply moved by what they had seen. It was left to the later generations among whom the legends of the saints proliferated to add the visible presence of angelic beings to the scenes.

It is not that the contemporary writers and the martyrs whose acts they chronicled did not believe in angels. It is to their dreams and visions we must turn, rather than to their outer experiences, to find how important the concept was to them in their spiritual lives. Fortunately, a few of these have been preserved.

Among the popular books that were widely circulated among Christians in the early centuries was *The Shepherd of Hermas*.[1] Written at Rome about the middle of the second century, it was read for many years in the churches before the order of public worship took the prescribed form it was later to assume. The book has been called a manual of personal religion, since it is clearly the expression of one man's experience as he undertook his own search for the Christian way of life. Although the identity of Hermas has not been verified from other sources, scholars generally agree that he was a real person, who, according to his own account, was neither bishop, priest, nor deacon, but an ordinary citizen who had started life as a slave. After he had been freed he had become prosperous, raised a family, and lost his wealth again. In purpose *The Shepherd of Hermas* resembles Bunyan's *Pilgrim's Progress*, and in its own time it probably held a place similar to that which the seventeenth-century allegory took in the Protestant world.

The book begins with a series of visions in which Hermas was instructed by a female figure, later identified as the Church. At first she appeared old (the Church had existed from the beginning), but as the writer gained in understanding and his spirit was renewed, she became younger. Hermas soon encountered angels, who appeared as young men attending the female figure, but it was not until the fifth vision that his own angelic guide appeared. As he sat on his bed in prayer, he became aware of the presence of "a man of glorious aspect, dressed like a shepherd, with a white goat's skin, a wallet on his shoulders and a rod in his hand." Hermas refers to him at first as "he to whom I had been entrusted," but later he speaks of him as "the angel of repentance." The image of the Good Shepherd, familiar to all Christians and usually identified with Christ, is not an exclusively Christian symbol. This figure not only had a long history in pre-Christian Judaism, but was known also to the Egyptians and the Greeks. The latter called him Poimandres, "the shepherd of men," who, as one of the aspects of Hermes leads them to enlightenment. Hermas the Roman seems to have been the first to identify this familiar figure with a member of the angelic host. That he does not represent Christ himself in these visions is evident from the shepherd's own statement that he has been sent by "a most venerable angel," probably the archangel Michael, who appears later in the book. That an angel should take a form so meaningful in the traditions of all the peoples from whom the members of the Christian church were drawn would have been no surprise to the readers of Hermas's own time. Even though the old gods had been banished, the universal symbols that furnish the inner world of man lived on and found new applications.

In the initial visions Hermas encountered another universal symbol, that of the great beast, and came safely past it because of his faith, "casting his fear upon the Lord." After witnessing the building of a tower, stone by stone, which took shape under the hands of the six attendant angels, Hermas heard from the shepherd an explanation of all that he had seen. He then received from him a series of commandments in regard to the Christian life, which form the central core of the book. In commandment six, the guide told him that there are two angels with every man, one of righteousness and one of evil, who will make themselves known by their works in his heart. It is not clear whether he identified the angel of evil with Satan, but the next commandment tells how to deal with the evil when it appears. "Fear the Lord," he said, "but fear not the devil; for fearing the Lord you will have dominion over the devil, for there is no power in him." This view of the ascendancy of good over evil, even in a world which the Apostolic Fathers said was ruled by Satan, must have struck an encouraging note in the minds of those who read the book. Since Hermas was a layman, not a theologian, he wrote of religious concepts as he had experienced them, and it is noteworthy that he saw no need for any form of exorcism such as his contemporary Justin suggested. A man's faith in the Lord was all-sufficient.

The commandments are followed by a series of "similitudes" or allegorical scenes which the shepherd put before Hermas. In one of these the archangel Michael appears beside a willow tree so huge that it overshadows mountains and plains. Like the shepherd, the tree is universal as an image that has been used in countless ways to express ideas that can be illustrated by its form, its growth, and its uses.

In this instance, the shepherd says, it stands for the law of God. It seems appropriate that the tree should be a willow, rooted in ground close to living water, spreading its branches widely, and dividing into innumerable small twigs and shoots that can be easily rooted. Michael cuts off twigs from the great willow and gives them to each one of a vast crowd assembled around it. These are the people who have already professed their belief in Christ. The spiritual state of each one will be judged by the condition of the twig he has received when it is returned to the archangel. Some of the shoots wither, others stay as they were, while still others put out new green growth. As the shepherd explains, Michael, the first of the archangels, has in his hands the government of all the people who have heard the proclamation of the Son of God and believed in him. Already the young Christian Church has claimed the guardian angel of the Hebrew people as its own.

The personal element that appears throughout *The Shepherd of Hermas* marks it as a genuine work inspired by inner experience. It matters little whether actual dreams or waking visions furnished its form, or whether it is the conscious creation of an imagination fired by new insight in a freshly awakened mind. Hermas as a person takes part in every scene as an observer, inquirer, and man whose conscience is aroused to a new sense of what it means to be a Christian. He sees that he has been too absorbed in business to conduct his family life as he should have done, and he takes upon himself the blame for the sins of his children. As the scenes progress, the reader can follow the signs of his changing spiritual condition. It is not until after the vision of Michael and the willow tree that his guide explains to him why the revelations came to him at first through the figure of the woman. Another universal symbol, the holy virgin, held a strong appeal to the early Christians. The concept was not yet concentrated into the person of the "Mother of God," the "Queen of Heaven." Virginity in itself was held in special esteem, and the many virgin saints who appeared in the early Christian era made no claim to a place in the celestial hierarchy. The holy virgin was a human being, with all the potentialities of power and meaning a woman carries for men, totally dedicated to the spiritual life. She represented the man's soul and could be for him a spiritual mother, guide, companion, and inspiration, without the encumbrance of the demands of the flesh. It was through her, the shepherd told Hermas, that he had to learn the lessons of the first visions, because he was as yet too weak spiritually to see the angel of the Lord. He was led gradually by means of this accessible human figure to the state in which he was able to apprehend the more glorious vision.

It was about half a century after *The Shepherd of Hermas* was written that the shepherd figure appeared again, in the dreams of a young woman who became a martyr at Carthage in the year 203. The personal record left by Perpetua gives the story of her inner experience while in prison awaiting death together with her maid Felicitas, who also remained "faithful to the end." [2] A young woman of twenty-two, married, and of good Roman family, Perpetua was a new convert to Christianity, a catechumen under the tutorship of a man named Saturus. Why she and a few other catechumens were arrested we do not know. The character of their teacher is revealed in his giving himself up voluntarily to share the fate of his pupils. Perpetua had a baby at the breast, and Felicitas was eight months pregnant. Her brother was also one of the group.

Perpetua kept a diary giving a lucid account of all that happened: of her devoted pagan father's efforts to persuade her to renounce her faith, not only for her own sake but for that of her child; of her talks with her brother; of her anxiety for her baby and her final relief when he no longer needed her breast and could be taken care of by others; of the examination and the sentence that was imposed on them all, condemning them to the beasts. It was with "great joy," she said, that they returned to the prison, knowing that they were to die. Her record ends: "Such were my doings up to the day before the games. Of what was done in the games themselves, let him write who will."

Perpetua's story must have made a deep impression on the Christians in her city, for her diary was edited after her death, and the story was completed by an able writer, possibly Tertullian. We learn that two days before the games Felicitas gave birth to a girl, whom one of the sisters adopted, and that Perpetua refused with such high spirit to change into the prescribed garments, the robes of the devotee of Ceres, that the two women were allowed to go into the arena in their own clothes. Perpetua's courage in meeting the mad heifer that was loosed upon them and her thoughtfulness for her weaker companion won her the admiration of the crowd, and she was finally allowed to die by the sword. Seeing the hesitation of the young swordsman as he approached her, she seized his hand and guided it herself to her throat. The editor concluded his account:

"Perhaps so great a woman, who was feared by the unclean spirit, could not otherwise be slain except she willed."

A large part of Perpetua's manuscript is taken up with a record of the dreams she had while in prison. They were far more important to her than the events and sufferings of her days, for she felt they were directly sent to her by God to give her courage and to prepare her for the future. Saturus also left a record of a dream, which the editor added to Perpetua's account when he completed the story of the passion of this little group. For the purpose we are pursuing here, we may concentrate on certain figures that appear in the dreams of both the pupil and the teacher. The contrast between the two persons—the young woman, newly converted to a religion that had seized her completely and produced in her an explosion of spiritual energy, and the older man, her teacher, long experienced in Christian discipline and modes of thought—is clearly reflected in their dreams. It is worthy of notice that each of them appears in the other's dream.

Perpetua's dream was as follows:

> I saw a brazen ladder of wondrous length reaching up to heaven, but so narrow that only one could ascend at once; and on the sides of the ladder were fastened all kinds of iron weapons. There were swords, lances, hooks, daggers, so that if anyone went up carelessly or without looking upwards he was mangled and his flesh caught on the weapons. And just beneath the ladder was a dragon crouching of wondrous size who lay in wait for those going up and sought to frighten them from going up. Now Saturus went up first, who had given himself up for

our sakes of his own accord, because our faith had been of his own building, and he had not been present when we were seized. And he reached the top of the ladder, and turned, and said to me, "Perpetua. I await you; but see that the dragon bite you not." And I said: "In the name of Jesus Christ he will not hurt me." And he put out his head gently, as if afraid of me, just at the foot of the ladder, and as though I were treading on the first step, I trod on his head. And I went up and saw a vast expanse of garden, and in the midst a man sitting with white hair, in the dress of a shepherd, a tall man, milking sheep; and round about were many thousands clad in white. And he raised his head and looked upon me, and said, "You have well come, my child." And he called me, and gave me a morsel of the milk [one translation uses "cheese"] which he was milking and I received it in my joined hands, and ate; and all they that stood around said "Amen." And at the sound of the word I awoke, still eating something sweet. And at once I told my brother, and we understood that we must suffer, and henceforth began to have no hope in this world.

This is the dream of Saturus:

Me thought we had suffered, and put off the flesh, and began to be borne toward the east by four angels whose hands touched us not. Now we moved not on our backs looking upward, but as though we were climbing a gentle slope. And when we were clear of the world below we saw a great light, and I said to Perpetua, for she was by my side: "This is what the Lord promised us, we have received his promise." And while we were carried by those four angels, we came upon a great open space, which was like as it might be a garden, having rose-trees and all kinds of flowers. The height of the trees was like the height of a cypress, whose leaves sang without ceasing. Now there in the garden were certain four angels, more glorious than the others, who when they saw us gave us honor, and said to the other angels, "Lo! They are come; lo! they are come," being full of wonder. And those four angels which bore us trembled and set us down, and we crossed on foot a place strewn with violets, where we found Jucundus and Saturninus and Artaxius, who were burned alive in the same persecution, and Quintus, who, being also a martyr, had died in the prison, and we asked of them where they were. The other angels said unto us: "Come first and enter and greet the Lord."

And we came near to a place whose walls were built like as it might be of light, and before the gate of that place were four angels standing, who as we entered clothed us in white robes. And we entered and heard a sound as of one voice saying: "Holy, holy, holy," without ceasing. And we saw sitting in the same place one like unto a man, white-haired, having hair as white as snow, and with the face of a youth; whose feet we saw not. And on the right and on the left four elders; and behind them were many other elders standing. And entering, we stood in wonder before the throne; and the four angels lifted us up, and we kissed Him, and He stroked our faces with His hand. And the other elders said to us: "Let us stand." And we stood and gave the Kiss of Peace. And the elders said to us: "Go and play." And I said to Perpetua: "You have your wish." And she said to me: "Thanks be to God, that as I was merry in the flesh, so am I now still merrier here."

And we went forth and saw before the doors Optatus the bishop on the right, and Aspasius the priest-teacher on the left, severed and sad. And they cast themselves at our feet, and said: "Make peace between us, for you have gone forth, and left us thus." And we said to them: "Are not you our father, and you our priest? Why should ye fall before our feet?" And we were moved, and embraced them. And Perpetua began to talk Greek with them, and we drew them aside into the garden under a rose tree. And while we talked with them, the angels said to them: "Let them refresh themselves; and if ye have any quarrels among yourselves, forgive one another." And they put those to shame, and said to Optatus: "Reform your people, for they come to you like men returning from the circus and contending about its factions." And it seemed to us as though they wished to shut the gates. And we began to recognize many brethren there, martyrs, too, among them. We were all fed on a fragrance beyond telling, which contented us. Then in my joy I awoke.

These dreams are not allegorical inventions, written to edify the readers, but real dreams of a man and a woman who knew they were soon to die. Such irrational details as the milking of cheese in Perpetua's dream and the elders' command to go and play in the dream of Saturus could only be products of the unconscious. In certain respects the two show similarities. Both dreamers move upward toward a heavenly garden, both find a central figure with white hair, and both awake with a sensation of sweetness—one as of taste, the other of fragrance. Each dreamer is aware of the other sharing the experience, each seeing the other in the dream in accordance with the real relation between them in life. Perpetua, still in the agony of fitting her spirit for the ordeal ahead of her, saw her teacher as her leader and guide, already at the top of the terrible ladder that must be ascended before the other world was reached.

Saturus was, in a sense, her guardian angel. He, on the other hand, saw the loved pupil whom he had himself converted as his companion on the heavenly journey after the suffering was over. In him the evils and the dangers of the way Perpetua had to pass had already been met, and the suffering of the final act of sacrifice was only a means to an end.

There is nothing markedly Christian in Perpetua's dream except the ceremonial morsel reminiscent of the Communion. The ladder, the dragon, the Good Shepherd could all have appeared in the dream of a pagan Greek, Roman, or Egyptian. She saw no angels of the Judaeo-Christian tradition, for her image of her teacher as the source of wisdom and spiritual support took their place. There is certainly a strong resemblance between her shepherd and that of Hermas, whose book she had undoubtedly read, but nothing in her description leads one to suppose she identified him either with Christ himself or one of the angels. He was a more general figure whose sole purpose in the dream seems to be to give the dreamer the morsel that is the sign of her admission to the company of the blest. Her dream was a direct psychic experience, lifting her to a new level of her spiritual being.

In contrast, Saturus was soaked in Christian doctrine and tradition. He and his companion were borne by angels (or enabled by them to float upwards) to the paradise in the east, where they saw a great light. From the garden they were conducted by a higher order of angels into the presence of the Lord himself. In each instance where angels are mentioned, they appear in fours, the number that forms the perfect square, a symbol of completion. The Lord's feet

were not seen, for feet are of the earth, and this was a
wholly spiritual being. The kiss with which they greeted
him and the elders who were present was a salutation into
which the early Christians had put new meaning. Stripped
of its sensual significance, it was a sign of their brotherhood
and had a definite place in their ritual. Saturus's familiarity
with the scriptures appears in such passages as the one in
which a voice chants, "Holy, holy, holy," as did the four
cherubim in the fourth chapter of Revelation. His sense of
responsibility for the Christian community in which he was
a leading layman is shown in the appeal made to him by the
quarreling bishop and priest whom he apparently had left
alive on earth. That these might have represented intracta-
ble elements in himself of which he had not been aware is
suggested by the way the matter was taken out of his hands
by the angels. He found that his busy concerns with the
affairs of his Church on earth had to give way in heaven to
a higher authority. After all, it had been his feminine side,
represented in Perpetua, who had attempted to reconcile
the men, speaking to them in Greek, a language foreign to
them all. Perhaps the angel's rebuke contained a message
concerning his own argumentativeness.

The angels in the dream of Saturus are strictly conventional in their activities. They conduct the souls of the dead
to heaven, they are keepers of the garden of Paradise, and
they guard the gate to the court of heaven. No single angel
is designated as a special guide or acts alone, but they always appear collectively. They are of different ranks, and
the conductors of souls tremble before the more glorious
keepers of the garden. There is no description given of
their appearance, and Christian art had not yet begun to

represent angels, but Saturus's dream would have lent itself well to a decorative treatment such as began to appear two centuries later. In spite of the ordered setting, it was a very personal heaven to which the martyr was introduced. He saw only a few angels, not ten thousand, and he recognized his friends one at a time. There were no streams of fire or thrones of precious stones, but the Lord stroked the faces of the two newcomers when they were lifted up to kiss him. Heaven was not a place of awesome majesty but one in which the merry soul of Perpetua could expand at ease. It was a comforting vision with which to face death in the arena. We are told that after the boar and the bear had failed to touch him, Saturus was mortally wounded by one bite of the leopard. Mindful to the end of his calling as a saver of souls, as his last act he asked for the ring from the finger of a soldier named Pudens who attended him, dipped it in his blood, and returned it to the owner "as a legacy," saying, "Farewell! Keep my faith and me in mind! And let these things not confound, but confirm you."

6 / WINGS AND NIMBUS

It would be interesting to know how the early Christians imagined angels. Through the first two centuries they had no religious art of their own from which to draw their ideas of the appearance of the celestial beings who were a part of their spiritual heritage. While the Fathers of the Church discussed the nature and attributes of angels, the more concrete minds of the laymen were left without a prescribed image around which to center their mental vision. Hermas saw his angelic guide in the guise of the Good Shepherd, dressed in a white goatskin, but he gave no description of the archangel Michael or the other angels who took part in his story. Saturus, the martyr, saw angels in his dream, but he did not describe them. Did they have wings? As the angels bore the souls to heaven, Saturus said only that they did not touch them with their hands but caused them to move upward as if they were climbing a gentle slope. How did he distinguish the angels from the elders who stood at the right and left of the Lord? The Lord himself he described as "one like unto a man, having hair as white as snow and with the face of a youth." Perpetua, too, saw the central figure in her dream as a man with white hair.

It is the quality of whiteness itself, representing light and purity rather than the venerableness of age, that seems most significant in these references to white hair. The association of whiteness with holiness was traditional in the Jewish culture from which Christianity sprang. The "shining robes" of the scriptures were echoed in the dream of Saturus when the angels clothed his soul and that of Perpetua in white robes before they passed into the holy presence. Presumably the angels themselves were similarly arrayed. The white robes, however, were not indispensable, if we judge by an example of contemporary Jewish art in the East. The remains of a synagogue, built at the small Roman outpost of Dura-Europos in Syria during the last half of the second century, contain a remarkable wall painting of Jacob's dream at Bethel. The figures ascending and descending the ladder above Jacob's head are dressed in full trousers tucked into high boots, and tunics with belts. Jacob himself wears Greek dress, as did most of the upper classes of the time, but the angels' costume probably represented the attire of court or temple guards.

In the same place, not far from the synagogue, archaeologists have unearthed the earliest Christian church that has yet been found. An inscription on its walls shows that it was either built in A.D. 233 or remodeled in that year, for it appears to have been adapted from its first use as a private house. During the first two centuries the Christian congregations were accustomed to meeting in the homes of the members, and little thought was given to decorations. If the owners were rich enough, their houses might be decorated in the prevailing secular style, with allegorical figures and naturalistic arrangements of fruit and flowers. At Dura-Europos, however, we find the beginnings of definitely Christian subject matter.

To be sure, the neighboring synagogue, which was built some years earlier, provided a model for the Christian brethren, many of whom may have been of Jewish ancestry. One can imagine that the small congregation did the best it could to make its meeting place as attractive as that of its more affluent neighbors. The wall paintings were similar to those in the synagogue, but the execution was less skillful. Like the Jews' paintings, they represented stories from the scriptures such as those of Adam and Eve and David and Goliath, but they included scenes representing the miracles of Jesus. The only symbolic figure now to be seen in the church is that of the Good Shepherd, at that time still the favorite symbol for the Savior. The cross had not yet undergone the transformation that turned it from an instrument of death by torture to a symbol of life and salvation. Missing also from this church are the angels. While the synagogue shows not only Jacob's booted and belted guardians but white-robed figures as attendants for Moses and other heroic figures, who show their detachment from the earthly scenes by their ceremonial gestures, the Christians made no attempt to represent spiritual

Babylonian cylinder seal, design similar to those from Ur, eighteenth century B.C. (Metropolitan Museum of Art, New York; Rogers Fund and Bequest of W. Gedney Beatty)

inged lion, gold Persian plaque, eighth tury B.C. (Metropolitan Museum of t, New York; Fletcher Fund and litzer Bequest)

ptian god Horus, as a hawk, c. eighth tury B.C. (Fogg Art Museum, Cam-dge, Mass. Bequest of Grenville L. nthrop)

Six-winged seraph, c. twelfth century, from the Church of Santa
Maria d'Aneu, Barcelona.

William Blake (1757–1827), "The Whirlwind: Ezekiel's Vision of Cherubim and Eyed Wheels." (Museum of Fine Arts, Boston)

Tobias and Raphael, from a Romanesque capital at Besse-en-Chandesse, Puy-de-Dôme, France. (Photo: Jean Roubier)

Rembrandt (1606–1699), detail from "Tobias and the Angel." (The Louvre, Paris)

Filippino Lippi (1457–1504), "Tobias and the Angel." (National Gallery of Art, Washington, D.C.; Samuel H. Kress Collection)

Jacob wrestling with the angel, from the *Vienna Genesis*, sixth century A.D. (Nationalbibliotek, Vienna)

The Good Shepherd and the vintage, from a fourth-century A.D. sarcophagus. (Lateran Museum, Rome; photo: Hirmer Fotoarchiv, Munich)

Apostle with martyr's crown, late fourt
century A.D., from the Baptistry of S
John, Naples. (Photo: courtesy Verla
Herder KG)

Perpetua and Felicitas, early sixth
century A.D., from Archepiscopal
Chapel, Ravenna. (Photos: courtesy
Verlag Herder KG)

beings. The time of the angels in Christian art had not yet come.

Before the beginning of the fourth century similar decorations using Biblical scenes began to appear in Christian meeting places at Rome as well as in the East. A large catacomb in the Via Latina, discovered in 1955 and dated about A.D. 300, contains many such wall paintings. In a curious combination of sacred and secular subjects, we find Adam and Eve, Abraham, Lot, and Balaam, together with allegorical figures of virtues and attributes, such as were currently used in non-Christian art, peacocks, *putti*, animals, and garlands of flowers, as well as a scene apparently depicting the death of Cleopatra. In this strangely mixed company we find our first angels. Abraham is seen receiving the three strangers under the oaks of Mamre, and they are shown as Abraham is said to have seen them, simply as three men. The tree under which they sat is there, and beside Abraham stands an animal that may be a sheep or the calf that was later to be sacrificed to entertain the strangers. There are no wings, no halos or other distinguishing features about the three guests. In the panels representing the story of Balaam, the angel who blocks the prophet's path wears a beard and carries a sword. There is nothing in his figure or equipment, which is strictly military, to suggest his celestial origin. In another panel Adam and Eve are being driven out of Paradise by a bearded giant, and in a painting of Jacob's dream one angel ascending the ladder and another descending appear as men in ordinary dress. Clearly the idea of attempting to represent a spiritual being in any special form of its own had not yet occurred to the Christian artists or the sponsors and authorities who commissioned their work. Since angels were supposed to be able to assume any form they chose, they were shown as they might have appeared to the actors in the stories illustrated.

It was in the reign of Constantine the Great, who ruled the Roman Empire from A.D. 306 to 337 and proclaimed Christianity the official religion, that Christian art began to flower, and it was in his time or shortly thereafter that the characteristic appearance of the Christian angels began to take form. It was at Constantine's capital, Byzantium, that the precedence was set for the wings that have been almost universally used since that time. The carved angels on a fourth-century child's sarcophagus in the Istanbul Archaeological Museum surprise us with their familiarity. These naturalistic flying figures might have been the work of a European artist of the sixteenth century. Although the arts of Byzantium were heavily influenced by those of Persia and other countries of the East, these early Christian winged angels are wholly in the Greek tradition and seem to have been taken over almost intact from the flying Nike figures that had come to be used decoratively on monuments to the great of the earth. Since Nike was a pagan deity, and a female one at that, the Christians modified their model so as to make it indistinguishable as to sex. Officially sexless, the angels of Byzantium were at least never feminine.

The conversion of Constantine is said to have been the result of a vision of a luminous cross in the sky, which led him not only to adopt Christianity but to undertake the military campaigns that brought him the supreme power in the empire. He was no saint and was certainly not a theologian, but he was an able administrator with a strong sense of justice. Under his rule persecutions ceased and the Church burst its shackles and began to move with vigor. A great wave of expansion resulted in the building of many churches and monasteries, not only in the Byzantine East but in Africa, Italy, Gaul, and even Britain and Ireland. A period of stormy theological arguments accompanied the expansion, and the Emperor, with his strong sense of unity and order, sought to settle it by calling together the first ecumenical congress at Nicaea in 325. It was the building of the churches that brought about the quite sudden emergence of distinctively Christian art, but it was the formulation of official Christian doctrine that produced the particular forms in which it appeared. In its development it reflected the shift of viewpoint in the Christian communities as doctrine and liturgy began to crystallize.

Questions concerning the nature of the historic Jesus, of the place of the Christ figure in the Trinity, of the function of the Holy Spirit in the soul of man, and of man's relation to the cosmos as a whole placed the individual Christian in a new light. Man was no longer seen as a completely earthly creature, such as the thought of the Old Testament writers had made him. The unity of the cosmos, to the ancient Hebrews, had been composed of two disparate parts; Yahweh was utterly distinct from man. But now, since God had entered man in the person of Jesus Christ and Christ had promised the indwelling Spirit to those who believed, a new unity was conceived of, in which man was lifted out of his condition of bondage to the earth and partook of the life of God. The Christian experience had brought him into a state which Charles Williams, in his book *The Descent of the Dove*, names "co-inherence." The distinction between body and soul, however, became even sharper than before, and the corporal man was denied any value, while the whole of Christian life was elevated to another and more spiritual plane. The earthly kingdom of Christ was no longer the goal; it was to life in heaven that man aspired.

As Christian places of worship increased and the authorities who caused them to be built sought new ways of decorating them, Hellenistic art, which had so long dominated, gave way before the change in man's view of himself in relation to his universe. C. R. Morey, in his *Early Christian Art*, says of this change:

> The shift of viewpoint thus connoted was fundamental; the world was to lose for Christian eyes its intrinsic beauty. Physical truth or ideal was to be no longer the conscious goal of art; nature was to become the medium for the portrayal of the supernatural, and painting and sculpture, from being the record of impressions from the world without, commenced their medieval role of conveying the expression of a transcendental world within the soul.[1]

For a long time in both East and West a distinction existed between the angels shown in scenes from the Bible and those that appeared as members of the heavenly host. In the remarkable mosaics of the Church of Santa Maria Maggiore in Rome, dating from the latter part of the fourth century or the first half of the fifth, both types are found. Following the tradition set by the early illustrations of the Greek translation of the Hebrew Bible called the Septuagint, the angels of the Old Testament stories are still seen without wings, but already realism is giving way to

Christian symbolism, and where the subject is related to Christ, angels with wings and nimbi hover in the background or take their places beside the human figures.

Even in the treatment of the scenes from the Old Testament, a difference has begun to appear. The three strangers whom Abraham received are still wingless and still wear white robes, but they are given nimbi. The central figure is placed within an ellipse in which radiating lines represent rays of light. Since the Church Fathers treated the Old Testament stories as allegories anticipating the doctrines of Christianity, this mandorla, a symbol of divinity, probably was meant to represent the Logos, who was believed to be part of the Godhead from the beginning. In the third of the three scenes depicted, where Abraham entertains his guests at the table, the mandorla is omitted, though the nimbus is still shown. Having served in the first scene to establish divinity, it may have seemed unnecessary or inappropriate in the purely human action of the last. The angel whom Joshua encountered outside the walls of Jericho is shown as a tall wingless figure, dressed for battle in a coat of mail and equipped for his mission with a long spear, but he is given a nimbus to distinguish him from the human warrior whom he has been sent to assist.

Authorities disagree as to whether or not there was a lapse of nearly a hundred years between this series of mosaics and another in the same church, representing Gospel scenes. Whether or not the second series was made at a later time, the difference of treatment is surely related to the subject matter and reflects the new trend away from earthly realism and toward an expression of the spiritual realities of the Christian experience. In the scene where an angel appears in a dream to Saint Joseph, to clear his doubts in regard to Mary after she was found with child, six angels take part in the scene. The speaker stands close to Joseph, four others stand with hands extended in a gesture of blessing, and the sixth hovers over Mary's head. Where Jesus is brought to the temple, winged angels are present in the background, as they are also in the scene of visit of the Magi, which does not take place in a stable with the infant Jesus lying in a manger. The earthly scene is wholly forgotten, and the figures are removed to the spiritual world, where the Christ Child is seated on a throne to receive the adoration of his visitors.

For people of later times, to whom such concepts as that of the Christ Child enthroned with angels in attendance are so familiar as to have become trite, it is hard to imagine how new and experimental early Christian art must have seemed. This is brought home to us by a letter written near the end of the fourth century that shows how much doubt still existed in the minds of Christian leaders concerning the right way to decorate the new churches. The writer was Saint Nilus, a monk of Sinai, to whom a bishop named Olympiodorus had turned for advice about the decoration of a church for which he was responsible. He wished to know whether it would be appropriate to conform to the current style and use hunting and fishing scenes to please the eye. No, said the saint, such a project would be useless and childish; what one should use in a church was the image of the cross, and on the walls should be painted scenes from the Old Testament and the Gospels, for the edification of the people.

Although innovations seem to have taken place in Rome and elsewhere, it was actually in the new Christian capital at Byzantium that Christian art first developed a definite and consistent style. There it was given official sanction and was a part of the general culture that grew up on the foundation of Greek civilization, modified by influences from the East. The already rich arts of Byzantium, which had been lavishly used for the glorification of the secular powers, were gradually turned toward the spiritual world. A number of symbols that later became a part of Christian iconography were first seen in the palaces and tombs of emperors and others to whom honor was due. Sometimes a circle of light surrounded the head of the person who was to be glorified, as later it was used to convey the sanctity of the saints and angels. The orb, a symbol of totality, which was carried by the emperor as a sign of his power, was surmounted in Christian times by the cross and placed in the hand of the archangel Michael. In the tombs of Palmyra as well as those of Byzantium, a portrait of the person to be honored had been placed in a frame upheld by four flying Nike figures. Following this idea, it came to be the custom in the Byzantine churches to have the circle in the center of the dome upheld by four flying angels, or surrounded by the four symbolic creatures taken over from the vision of Ezekiel to represent the four evangelists.

The Byzantine state understood itself to be the replica on earth of the kingdom of Christ in heaven. However far it may have strayed from the path of Christian virtue, it had no other constitution than the four Gospels, and the emperor was the representative of Christ in the material world. He was not considered divine, as the pagan emperors had been, but the position he occupied was invested with such majesty as could only be accorded to one whose authority was delegated by divinity. It is no wonder that grandeur is the foremost quality of Byzantine art.

Church and state together were built on a pattern of symbolism, from the ceremonial acts surrounding the throne in the palace to the liturgy before the altar in the church. Each part of the church building itself held its special symbolic meaning, and the decorations were consistent with it. It came to be such a convention to assign certain subjects to certain places on the walls and vaults and to represent them in such specific ways that manuals were written for the use of artists, to be followed in detail. By the time Byzantine art became a fixed style, a hierarchic order prevailed in the mural decorations. In the lowest rank were the saints and martyrs, and above them appeared scenes from the Gospels. The apse was assigned to the Virgin, and her figure was usually placed between the archangels Michael and Gabriel. The dome was reserved for the heavenly court, with Christ in the center, sometimes represented only by the symbol of the cross within a circle, surrounded by the figures of apostles and angels. The angels in these frescoes and mosaics, especially those of the sixth century, when the new style was at the height of its freshness and vigor, are imposing figures of masculine authority and intelligence. Their faces, flanked by powerful sweeping wings, often show such strongly individual character that they seem like portraits of known persons, yet their stiffly conventional poses keep them impersonal and remote from the world of men. Their place is wholly in the transcendental sphere, as courtiers in the kingdom of Christ to which the inner drama of Christian experience had been projected.

Wherever the culture of the Byzantine Empire was felt, these stately figures were seen, and they set a pattern that endured, especially in the East, for hundreds of years. As the power of the earthly Church increased, its recognized guardian, the archangel Michael, was portrayed with greater frequency. The classical white garments of the angels gradually gave way to robes of the court, studded with jewels; wings took on brilliant colors; the imperial purple was reserved for Christ himself. The whole spiritual realm became more and more a static picture of sublimity, while man was left to struggle in the material world, in which he met more demons than angels.

The Christian art of Western Europe was of course greatly influenced by the Byzantine style. Some of the finest and purest examples appeared in the mosaics of Sicily and at Ravenna, for a time the capital of the Western Empire, but it seems fitting that at Rome, which had so long dominated the world, this influence should be less strongly felt. The churches of Rome continued largely to follow their own traditions and to create new ones. Only in the Eternal City is it now possible to observe the steady development of Christian art during the centuries we call "dark." Waves of invasion. from north, east, and south were passing over Germany, France, Spain, and the British Isles. In the time of confusion, when political and social forces caused the retreat of traditional learning into the monasteries and limited the scope of Christian art, the Romans continued to build churches and to decorate them in their own way.

The Old Testament scenes became less common after the sixth century, whereas the saints and martyrs were given more importance. Angels had a part not only in the Gospel scenes in which they were said to have appeared, but as celestial presences in the adoration of the Virgin and Child and the glorification of the saints and martyrs. There is considerable diversity and freedom of style in the rendering. Individual artists brought their imagination into play to produce variations in form and color, but the main characteristics of angel representation were now set. Long, sweeping wings had become a part of the recognized pattern, and the nimbus was uniformly used. The white classical costumes gradually gave way to draperies of less definite outline, or, possibly under Byzantine influence, to ankle-length straight garments of rich material. However they might be dressed, the angel faces throughout the first millennium of Christian art remained strongly masculine, even when grace and freedom of movement marked a particular artist's work. Flying in space, forming a background for the divine figures in heaven, or attending the saints in their perilous lives or their places of glory after death, the angels were omnipresent and must have been as real to the worshipers who knelt in the churches as were the Holy Family and the martyrs whose legends were a part of the Christian heritage.

7 / THE AGE OF LEGEND

I arise today:
*   in the might of the Cherubim;*
*   in obedience of Angels;*
*   in ministration of Archangels;*
— SAINT PATRICK

Such a tangle of legends has gathered around the first millennium of Christianity that the persons who made Christian history and the masses who followed them seem shrouded in a colorful but obscuring web. In a world without print, where only a few could read and write, systematic records of facts scarcely existed. The effect of a person's life on his environment was what determined the way he was remembered—as indeed is largely the case today, for human beings have changed but little. The intangible and the unprovable carry the greatest weight when the past is transmitted to later generations by direct communication in speech. Assumptions made on the slenderest basis of fact grow in the next stage of a legend's development into something quite other than the original statement of what happened. The process starts with amazing promptness after the death of a person who has made an impression upon the life of his time, and sometimes even while he still lives. Going through several phases in as many centuries, the story not only becomes embellished with the incidents that seem most appropriate to each narrator, but may turn into a wholly new tale with a different set of characters.

This curious but persistent concomitant of history is certainly not to be disparaged because of its unreliability as fact. It springs from sources deeply embedded in the mind of man, which are touched by the qualities he perceives in his heroes and heroines, and it expresses the values and meanings held most dear by the people through whom it is passed on. When a young girl, fired by her faith in a religion that values purity, is persecuted to death because of her refusal to make a socially desirable marriage, her heroic virginity soon becomes surrounded by a supernatural aura. The story of Saint Agnes is an example.

A girl of thirteen, with parents whose names are known, and whose grave still exists, marked with her name, died at Rome in 305 as a result of tortures inflicted upon her. According to the Jesuit scholar Hippolyte Delahaye, within a century after her death several different stories about her were current, some of which contradicted one another. In general, the legend tells that Agnes refused an offer of marriage to a young man of high rank, that as a result she was sent to a brothel, from which she escaped, only to be seized and tortured to death. Legend adds that Agnes was met at the door of the brothel by an angel, who filled the place with light and protected her from all evil; that when the young lover tried to approach her he was stricken and died;

that the young man's father, by whose power she had been placed in the house of ill fame, then besought her prayers; and that, as a result of the son's restoration to life, both father and son accepted the Christian faith. The guilt of Agnes's death is placed, in the legend, on the pagan priests, who were enraged at this demonstration of Christian power. At first she had several miraculous escapes through the intervention of her guardian angel, but she at last succumbed when a sword was thrust down her throat. The details of the story varied in the different versions, but in all of them the sainthood of Agnes was enhanced by the multiplication of her sufferings and the miracles that attended her brief journey through life.

The theme of the holy virgin was one of the favorites of the early Christian centuries, and it appeared in many places and attached to many names. Stories similar to that of Agnes appeared under the names of such virgin saints as Agatha, Barbara, Cecilia, Dorothy, Margaret, and many others. Something of the supernatural appeared in each of them, and the angels were seen in their functions of guardian, messenger, and minister. Delahaye is inclined to dismiss the accounts of torture that seem to him excessive, and the miraculous escapes that delighted the hearers, as the mere imaginings of untutored minds or the inventions of the pious monks who recorded the stories for the purpose of instilling virtue in the hearts of the people; but the heart is similarly moved in priest and peasant, and a monk alone at his writing desk may be expressing an inner truth when he lets his imagination fill in the details of the picture of the dimly known figure he is trying to describe. There exists, to be sure, a natural craving for excitement that may be satisfied in various ways. In a world in which good and evil are inextricably mixed, the response to a tale of torture may be less an impulsion toward virtue than a vicarious outlet for violence, and the miraculous escape may appeal more to the instinct of self-preservation than to the need to recognize the power of God. Yet these Christian legends, like the older myths of earlier religions, contain central truths and a set of basic values that make them the expression of a particular way of life and attitude of mind.

Through many of the legends runs the angel theme, connecting God and man. Although later scholars have traced the beginnings of monasticism to a gradual development and its rules to a process of experiment, Palladius, writing a century after the founding of the first Coptic monastery by Pachomius, tells of the call the latter received through an angel to collect the young monks about him into a community. The rule for their communal life, he said, was given to Pachomius by the angel, inscribed on a brass tablet. The writer is expressing his reverence for the monastic way of life, and his belief in its authenticity as a God-given institution.

Despite the martyrdoms, the burning of books, and the destruction of churches—or perhaps, to a certain extent, because of them—Christianity continued to spread. Like seed borne on the wind, it had already been planted before the time of Constantine in every part of the Roman Empire. Throughout the Mediterranean lands and northward, through Gaul and Britain, the Christians carried with them such elements of their religion as they had absorbed. Gathering around them as they went, the mass of legends grew, and in the little centers of piety and learning among the forests and on lonely islands, old ones were cherished and new ones were made. Freshly converted pagans, bringing into their Christian life remnants of ancient traditions and half-forgotten myths of the old gods, added their share to the tangle of Christian lore.

Occasionally a man or woman would appear whose character shone like a point of light among the shadows of ignorance, unrest, and brutality in his environment and whose personality lent itself especially to the formation of legends. Such a one was Patricius, the native of Britain who became the much-loved Saint Patrick of Ireland. To his name clings such a collection of legends that Church authorities ever since have been trying to clear away the fabulous and reveal the real man. Patrick's own account of his life is as direct and simple as anyone could ask, even though his omissions have left the way open for others to fill in the missing years and circumstances by inference or in imagination. Matters of when and where were of little concern to Patrick, for it was the spiritual content of a man's life, not the sum of its events, that he found important.

So conscious still is Ireland of its principal saint that it is hard to realize how far in the past he walked through that green and gray land. While he encountered its kings and druids and organized the scattered Christians that already were there, struggling against heavy odds to live according to their faith, some of the Church's greatest thinkers were preaching and writing in the centers of Roman civilization. Although somewhat older than Patrick, Saints Ambrose, Augustine, Jerome, and John Chrysostom were all alive during his lifetime. Constantine had declared Christianity the official religion of the empire only sixty years or so before his birth, and while he was a young man of twenty-one Rome had fallen to the barbarians under Alaric.

Regardless of its other aspects, Saint Patrick's life was full of material for a rousing story of adventure. Born into a well-to-do Christian family somewhere on the west coast of Britain, he was seized by pirates at sixteen and carried into serfdom in Ireland. During the seven years he spent as swineherd to the chieftain Miliucc (or Milchu) he endured many lonely vigils, out of which came a spontaneous and intense religious experience. It was then that he began to notice his dreams and to find guidance from them. His account of his eventual escape does not attribute it to the intervention of angels, but the unexplained voice he heard gave him explicit directions, which he was able to follow quite literally, traveling to the south of Ireland to find the ship that was to carry him overseas. Coming upon traders who were sailing for Gaul with a cargo of wolfhounds, he was at first denied passage but was taken on at the last moment to help care for the lively and possibly vicious animals. On landing, he wandered for days without food in wild country, but finally found a monastery where he spent some years before returning to his family in Britain.

It was while Patrick was wandering in the forests of Gaul that he encountered Satan in a dream. "He fell upon me," he wrote, "as it were a huge rock, and I had no power over my limbs. But whence did it occur to me—to my ignorant mind—to call upon Helias [sic]? And on this I saw the sun rise in the heavens, and while I was shouting

'Helias' with all my might, the splendour of that sun fell upon me and straightway shook all weight off me. And I believe I was helped by Christ the Lord, and that the Spirit was even then calling aloud on my behalf."

Here is Patrick, the ardent Christian, a refugee from slavery, dreaming in the wilderness of the forces of darkness and light and summoning from an unknown source within himself the same symbol that he had probably seen worshiped by the druids in Ireland. Surprised as we all are at the contents of our dreams, he heard himself using the Greek word (which in his "ignorant mind" he misspelled) and finding deliverance in his instinctive appeal to the sun, which on waking he immediately identified with the only power to which he gave allegiance, Jesus Christ.

The next and most important dream that Patrick recorded occurred after his return to Britain some years later. There he was joyfully received by his kindred and urged to wander no more, but again an inner authority spoke, which he could not disobey. This is his own account of the dream:

> And there verily I saw in the night visions a man whose name was Victoricus coming as it were from Ireland with countless letters. And he gave me one of them, and I read the beginning of the letter, which was entitled "the Voice of the Irish," and while I was reading aloud the beginning of the letter, I thought that at that very moment I heard the voice of them who lived beside the Wood of Foclut which is nigh unto the western sea. And thus they cried, as with one mouth, "We beseech thee, holy youth, to come and walk among us once more." And I was broken

[99

in heart, and would read no further. And so I awoke. Thanks be to God, that after very many years the Lord granted to them according to their cry.[1]

The messenger in this dream, in contrast to the supernatural figure of Satan in the previous one, is described simply as "a man." It is only his name, Victoricus, that adds a dream quality to his presence, for the Latin name should be simply "Victor," and the extra syllables seem to be a variation irrationally added. We have no idea whether Patrick ever knew such a man in reality, or whether this was one of those figures arising spontaneously from the unconscious that represent an unknown aspect of the dreamer's own being. To Patrick's earliest biographers the messenger was without question an angel, and these writers of the seventh century were doubtless following still earlier authorities, who had gathered the local traditions that had sprung up wherever he passed, and had drawn their own conclusions. The angel Victoricus became an entity to all who loved the memory of Saint Patrick.

It is not of great importance whether Patrick himself thought of Victoricus as an angel. The message he brought was in any case God-given as Patrick saw it, and to fulfill the call became his aim, although it was at least twenty years before he was able to carry out the plan to return to Ireland. He would not go until he was deemed worthy of a commission from the church authorities, which, after years of study in the monasteries of Auxerre and Lerins, came to him in the form of a papal appointment as bishop.

It was a rough life that Patrick lived in Ireland among the warring clans with their inflated sense of glory and their violent loves and hates. Something of their pride is shown in the story of Miliucc, to whom he had once been a slave. When all Ireland was turning to Christianity under Patrick's powerful influence, Miliucc resisted to the end. Rather than submit and confess his faith, it is said, he set fire to his house and destroyed himself with all his possessions. Patrick admitted in his "Confession" that he was often homesick, and indeed he seems to have had no settled home in Ireland but was constantly moving from place to place in his turbulent see. The stories that grew up about his acts in every place he visited are as full of demons as they are of angels. It is no wonder that in the beautiful hymn known as the "Lorica" or breastplate of Saint Patrick, one stanza is an invocation to all the forces of heaven and nature to protect him from the evils he found around him.

> I invoke all these forces:
> between me and every savage force that may
> come upon me, body and soul;
> against incantations of false prophets;
> against black laws of paganism;
> against false laws of heresy;
> against idolatry;
> against spells of women and smiths and Druids;
> against all knowledge that should not be known.[2]

The seventh-century biographer Muirchu assumed that the angel Victoricus was with Patrick from the beginning of his religious life during his serfdom. He even claimed that the angel visited him "on every seventh day of the week; and as one man talks with another, so Patrick enjoyed the angel's conversation." This may not be far from the truth, for some men who are sensitive to the movements within their own inner depths find there a seemingly separate personality to whom they can turn for wisdom greater than their consciousness is capable of. In the book *Experiment in Depth* P. W. Martin describes this helpful figure as experienced by certain persons in all cultures, from that of the Greeks of the classical period to that of the American Indians.

> This figure is variously named: it is Hermes, the messenger of the gods; it is the *psychopompus*, the way-shower, the conductor of souls, as Virgil conducted Dante in the infernal regions; it is the *daimon* on which Socrates placed his trust, the figure of the *genius* to the Romans, the "angel of the Lord" of the Hebrew scriptures, the guardian angel of Christian belief.[3]

The place in Ireland most reverently regarded because of its association with the country's patron saint is the mountain near the wild northwest coast known as Croagh Patrick. What really happened to Saint Patrick on its summit historians are unable to tell, for the legends have taken it over. The saint was nearing the end of his life, and he had seen Christianity established in every part of the country. Accompanied by some of his disciples, he is said to have climbed the mountain: some say to spend Holy Week, others the whole forty days of Lent. The main theme of the legends is constant, though the details vary. Patrick had a plea to put before his Lord, and there was a great striving on the mountaintop, in which the angel Victoricus took the part of messenger and mentor. Muirchu, who does not associate the foretelling of Patrick's death with the mountain at all, but does record the visit of Victoricus at that time, says that the saint prayed to be allowed to go to Armagh to die, for as the center of the religious life in Ireland it was the place he loved the most. This petition was denied. He was to return to the small place near the east coast where he had made his first convert, Dichu, and established his first church in an old barn. His other petitions, however, were granted: "That his jurisdiction be in Armagh; that on his death-bed he should judge the repentance of anyone who sang his hymn; that the descendants of Dichu have mercy; that at the Day of Judgment he should judge those to whom he was an apostle."

Other versions make the petition less personal and build up the scene to include all the saints of Ireland "past, present, and to come," in a sort of apotheosis of the whole body of Irish Christianity. The poet Aubrey de Vere, who put the old Irish legends into verse, probably used as his main outline the account that was most generally accepted by tradition. In the *argument* at the beginning of the poem "The Striving of St. Patrick on Mt. Cruachan," he says:

> St. Patrick, seeing that now Erin believes, desires that the whole land stand fast in belief till Christ returns to judge the world. For this end he resolves to offer prayer on Mt. Cruachan; but Victor, the Angel who has attended him in all his labours, restrains him from that prayer as being too great. Notwithstanding, the Saint prays three times on the mountain, and three times all the demons of Erin contend against him, and twice Victor, the Angel, rebukes his prayers. In the end St. Patrick scatters the demons with ignominy, and God's Angel bids him know that his prayer hath conquered through constancy.[4]

The legends about Saint Patrick grew out of the love the people had for him. Some of the accounts of his miracles, as

Oliver St. John Gogarty says in his book *I Follow St. Patrick*, tell of acts a Christian would not have committed, but show how the people felt about his power. In this greatest scene of all, when Patrick was striving with God, one is reminded of Jacob's all-night struggle with the angel, but such is the reverence of the people for their special saint that Patrick himself becomes the victor. Perhaps it is true that in this final inner crisis, whatever the nature of his prayers may have been, the man and his inner friend and guide, the angel Victoricus, were merged into one.

8 / GOOD AND EVIL IN THE MIDDLE AGES

At Lucifer, though he an angel were,
And not a man, at him I will beginne.
— CHAUCER

During the turbulent times in which feudalism was becoming a recognized pattern of society, security was represented on one side by the castle and on the other by the
Church. Between these two seats of power the masses lived
their precarious and largely illiterate lives. Their religious
views were a medley of remnants of pagan and folk myth,
such classical elements as had filtered down to them, and
Christian doctrine as it was preached by the priests and
monks who took an active part in the life around them.

Everyone, from princes to peasants, believed in demons
and attributed to them, under the power of Satan, most evil
happenings. Since the earth was considered to be the property of Satan, and the demons inhabited the lower air, the
forces of evil had much easier access to the world of man

than did the forces of good as represented by the nine ranks of celestial beings in the hierarchy of heaven. While the minds of a few scholars and intellectuals versed in classical modes of thought were engaged in speculating on the plan of the universe, the writings of one man became to Christians generally the authoritative source of knowledge on the form and structure of the heavenly court. Known as the Pseudo-Dionysius, because his treatises were first thought to have been the work of Dionysius the Areopagite, a convert of Saint Paul, this writer was probably a Syrian of the sixth century. His books were first translated into Latin from their original Greek in 860 and rapidly took the place in the Western countries that they had already occupied in the East. *The Celestial Hierarchy* and *The Ecclesiastical Hierarchy* not only gave names, positions, and functions to the angelic hosts, but built up a structure that made the Church on earth the counterpart of the court in heaven. Bringing together elements from the various traditional Jewish and Christian schools of thought, these writings formed a scheme that spoke with authority satisfying to medieval minds, whose thinking was marked by a longing for order and system. The unknown writer's three-times-three ranks of heavenly beings fitted well with the doctrine of the Trinity and became a part of the official teaching of the Church through many centuries.

While the cherubim, seraphim, and thrones, the dominions, virtues, and powers, and, closest to man, the princedoms, archangels, and angels remained in their immutable places, the kingdom of Satan contained no such formal organization. The earth itself and man's life on it saw to that, and although there may have been different classes of demons, the general impression was one of chaos. By long inheritance from the ancient civilizations of the East combined with tales of the earthly and even subterranean monsters of Northern tradition, the demons seem to have come into their own and proliferated in medieval times.

They were omnipresent. Since they could transform themselves into any form they chose, they were frequently seen as dogs, cats, or other animals, or else might appear in some alluringly deceptive guise as human or supernatural beings. The monasteries, which acted as islands of safety and light in a world of physical danger and moral obscurity, were particularly susceptible to their assaults, because it was there the powers of evil were most threatened by the earnestness of virtuous men. There is no one who is more in danger from demons than a would-be saint. When the monastery choir sang off key, it was the devil who had got them by the throat, and if a monk in his cell found his mind straying from his orisons, Satan was present with destructive intent. The everlasting conflict between good and evil in the souls of men was probably never seen in such concrete terms at any other period in history.

There are many stories of women who were violated by demons. Merlin, the prophet of the Britons, was said to have been born of an incubus demon and a nun. Caesarius, the prior of Heisterbach in the thirteenth century, in his great collection of incidents of the spiritual life called *The Dialogue on Miracles*, gives an account of how the devil is invoked by a necromancer and how he may be controlled by use of a magic circle. He tells of a knight who refused to believe in the existence of demons until he tried an experiment with the aid of a necromancer. Safe within the magic circle, the knight experienced frightening sights and sounds and carried on an interview with the devil himself, who finally convinced the knight of his reality by telling him in detail when and where he had committed certain sins.[1]

Satan was more real to the people of those times than was God the Father, and the force they felt emanating from him produced strange aberrations in their theological ideas. A theory that was popular in the early Middle Ages, though not sanctioned by the best minds, turned the doctrine of the atonement into a bargain with Satan, to whom, because of his claim to ownership of the earth, Christ was offered as ransom for the souls of men. The position of Satan in the doctrine of the church was not new. All the early Fathers had declared him the author of evil, though there were differences of opinion as to when and why he fell from his high place in heaven, and as to whether he was capable of redemption. It was not until medieval times, however, that he was identified with Lucifer, the morning star. It is not clear when or where the idea originated, but it was enunciated by Peter Lombard, one of the first doctors of theology at the University of Paris, in the twelfth century. He interpreted the passage in the fourteenth chapter of Isaiah, prophesying the overthrow of the king of Babylon, as a reference to Satan: "How art thou fallen from Heaven, O thou day-star, son of the morning! How art thou cut down to the ground, that dost lay low the nations!" This is part of a long diatribe against the oppressors of the Hebrew people. In characteristic medieval fashion, Peter Lombard removed the passage from its historical setting and interpreted it in theological terms. The name Lucifer remained for centuries synonymous with that of Satan.

It could almost be said that the people of the Middle Ages were fascinated by the personality of Satan. As Lucifer, he had been the highest and most beautiful of the angels before the fall that was the result of his arrogance. He was still able, in his pride as lord of the material world, to allure and entice men and women into sin. To be fascinated is a condition not only of being attracted to an object, but of being pulled toward it against one's will, even though everything in one revolts in terror. The Lucifer aspect of Satan, by its identification with the morning star, drew into its orbit all that was most appealing in earthly desires, while Satan in his other aspect of tormentor threatened to carry out the punishment in hell that would be exacted by God himself from those who fell into his clutches. The sinners seen in the carvings on Romanesque churches are being thrust by the angels through the gate of hell, to be met by the teeth and claws of the demons who live there. To be both the tempter and the punisher confers a power that is almost inescapable. The conviction that Satan is looking over every man's shoulder would be a source of constant anxiety if the human mind were not capable of living on more than one level at a time.

Saints, philosophers, and wise men of all times and persuasions have pointed out that evil is indeed present in all life and must somehow be dealt with. Perhaps the people of the Middle Ages were fortunate in being able to ascribe it to the existence of a single and definite entity. Looking back from the twentieth century, Freud in *Civilization and Its Discontents* said of the devil that belief in him was "the best way out in acquittal of God" for those who try to "reconcile the undeniable existence of evil with His omnipotence and supreme goodness." [2]

One way to deal with inescapable problems is to dramatize them, so that they can be seen in concrete terms. This the people of the later medieval times were able to do in the miracle and mystery plays that could be seen in every village, bringing before the audiences in living form all the elements of their religious faith and of the spiritual struggles of human existence. One of the best known of the English plays, *The Mystery of the Redemption* (sometimes called the *Ludus Coventrae*), in spite of the date of the manuscript, 1468, is said to have been drawn from earlier sources, and so can be seen as representative of the thought of preceding centuries. It gives the whole story of sin and redemption, from the creation to the Resurrection, and Satan plays an important part in it. His description of himself in the prologue to the second act presents him as the tempter. If a bit of comedy lurks in the lines, especially those drawing attention to his foppish costume, it only serves to heighten the effect of his outrageous exhortation. After all, the tempter's power may be reduced if he can be made to look ridiculous.

> I am your Lord Lucifer; from hell I came;
> Prince of this world and great duke of hell.
> So Satan is now my rightful name.
> I am come to hail you, and to greet you well.
> I am the nourisher of sin to confusion of man;
> To bring him to my dungeon to dwell in fire.
> To reward my servant is my princely plan;
> He shall sing my sad praises in hell's choir.
> Pay good heed to your prince, my people dear;

See what sports in heaven I dared to play.
To win a thousand souls an hour is a trifle here
Since I won Adam and Eve on the first day. . . .
See the ingenuity of my chequered disguise,
My garments fitting naturally together.
Each part correct in cut and size
From the sole of my foot to my bonnet's feather.
My long pointed shoes of the finest leather
With crimson stockings are my greatest joy;
My twenty points of lace tied with a liver tether
Make that gentleman yonder look like a boy.
I have long locks on my shoulders dangling down
To harbor live beasties that tickle men by night,
With a high bonnet for covering my crown;
I hold all beggars and poor men in despite.
In great oaths and lechery set your delight,
And maintain your estate by bribery and dinners;
If the law reprove you, say you will fight,
And gather a crowd of congenial sinners.
I have brought you new names where the old ones tire.
And since sin is so pleasant and each man's right,
You shall name pride honor, lust natural desire,
And covetousness wisdom, where money shines bright;
Wrath shall be called manhood, punishment called spite;
Perjury be a leader in each court or session;
Gluttony be called rest, abstinence be out of sight,
And all who preach virtue be put under repression.[3]

The other aspect of Satan, the ruler not of earth but of
hell, is seen with horrifying clarity in Dante's *Inferno*. In
his visions of the spiritual world, where past, present, and
future events were shown to him in one vast perspective,
Dante saw Satan as he was to be at the end of time, when

Christ's final triumph was to bring him to everlasting punishment. In the lowest circle of hell, consisting not of fire but of ice, "There where the frozen spirits as in glass/ Were covered wholly," the gigantic figure of "The Emperor of the kingdom of despair" was found encased up to the breast in a frozen prison.

> If he once was fair as he now is foul,
> And 'gainst his Maker dared his brows to raise,
> Fitly from him all streams of sorrow roll.

Three pairs of great bats' wings, still moving above the ice, blew frosty winds from each of the three faces of the giant's head that rose from his bare shoulders.

> At each mouth he was tearing with his teeth
> A sinner, as in flax by heckle frayed;
> Each of the three of them so suffereth.[4]

The three sinners were Judas Iscariot, Brutus, and Cassius. In his eternal punishment Satan was still used by God for the punishment of the world's great betrayers.

To emerge from hell, Dante and his guide Virgil had to pass through the very nadir of the celestial sphere, the lowest point in all the universe, where Satan in his humiliation was imprisoned. To reverse their direction and to rise again on the other side, where they would find the sea that contains the island of Purgatory, it was necessary for them actually to clamber down the hairy side of the monstrous form as if it had been a mountain. The mere sight of the author of evil in all the horror of his appearance was not enough: the soul's journey required a personal encounter, in which the evil thing itself was the means of approaching the way that would eventually lead them to heaven.

Such visions as came to Dante were not given to many, and ordinary people were more aware of Satan through his works in the visible world of sense. As prince of the demons, he was responsible for many of their physical ills, as well as for the sins to which he tempted them. Magic in various forms played an important role in medieval life, at a period when ancient beliefs and folklore from pre-Christian times still clung to the minds of the people. Witches and sorcerers who practiced the black arts were thought to have entered into personal relations with Satan, who no longer inhabited the lowest part of heaven but was an earthly presence, manifesting himself in countless ways. It was only in the churches that men and women could escape from his influence. Every community had at its center a fortress of God, where evil spirits could not enter. Here Christ was king, and although Satan might rule elsewhere, the mass and the sacraments that were celebrated in the church worked directly for the salvation of the penitent souls that took part in them. Not only was the church a symbol of the kingdom of heaven: it was a place of refuge and healing in the struggle of life. Even the church bell had its role in providing a place of safety; for as far as it could be heard, evil would flee when its voice rang out. This belief in the power of the church bell endured to much later times in places where remnants of paganism lingered. The folk tales of Norway tell of persons who had been bewitched and carried off to the stronghold of the trolls, but who were released by the ringing of the church bell if they were within earshot of its beneficent sound.

Preoccupation with the forces of evil did not altogether obscure the vision of heaven and its inhabitants, but it is hard to tell how much the idea of angel intervention meant to the ordinary layman in the Middle Ages, since few records of personal experience were kept except among the members of religious orders. Caesarius of Heisterbach includes in his *Dialogue on Miracles* a few accounts of visions of angels that had been told to him directly or by monks who had heard them from someone close to the source. It seems to have been to the simple-minded, the very old, the devout, or contrite women, and the dying that angels most often manifested themselves. The idea of the angels as the conveyors of souls to heaven was very popular, and when death occurred in a monastery the angels were sometimes seen and heard by more than one person. Those who were nearing death often heard angelic music. There was a longing among the pious for such perfection as could only be found in Paradise, so that saintly persons sometimes expressed openly their desire for death. One of these was Christina of Volmuntsteine, who, as Caesarius relates, saw in an ecstasy during Lent "a very majestic being, whose beauty was past all imagining." He told her he was the archangel Michael, whose duty it was to present the souls before God, and that her wish for death would be granted at Eastertime. The archangel's prediction came true, and who is to doubt it? Whether the wish brings its own fulfillment or whether through some faculty usually obscured a person may foresee his own death, no one would dare to say, but such cases are not unknown today.

It is noticeable that the stories Caesarius tells of the active intervention of angels in the affairs of men are less carefully documented than those of the visions. Although these events were supposed to have occurred in his own time,

Jacob's dream, third century A.D., from the synagogue at Dura-Europos, Syria. (Photo: Dura-Europos Publications)

Child's sarcophagus, fourth century A.D. (Archaeological Museum, Istanbul; photo: Hirmer Fotoarchiv, Munich)

The hospitality of Abraham, fifth century A.D., from the Church of Santa Maria Maggiore, Rome. (Photo: Alinari)

Christ, angels, and two saints, sixth century A.D., from the Church of San Vitale, Ravenna. (Photo: Alinari)

The Archangel Michael, leaf of diptych, sixth century A.D. (British Museum, London)

Saint Agnes, sixth century A.D., fr[om] the Church of San Apollinare N[u]ovo, Ravenna. (Photo: court[esy] Verlag Herder KG)

The Crucifixion, Irish bronze plaque, eighth century A.D. (National Museum of Ireland, Dublin)

Three devils seizing a soul, from
Romanesque capital at Besse-en-
Chandesse, Puy-de-Dôme, France
(Photo: Jean Roubier)

Fighting angel, from a Romanesque capital at Perrécy-les-Forges,
France. (Photo: Jean Roubier)

Souls of the chosen being brought to Abraham by angels, c. 1230, from a tympanum of Reims cathedral, France. (Photo: Martin Hürlimann)

Two angels with the Tree of Life, twelfth century, from west façade of the Cathedral of St. Pierre, Angoulême, France. (Photo: Archives Photographiques, Paris)

Smiling angel, thirteenth-century jamb figure from left porch of
Reims cathedral, France. (Photo: Martin Hürlimann)

they have the character of legend. A special aura of enchantment pervades the tales of miraculous events connected with the Crusades, which gained added credibility from having taken place in strange and distant lands. One such tale, told as if it were recent news from the war front, concerns six Knights Templars who were surprised at their prayers by a band of Saracens. When the leader of the knights told them to lie still and continue to pray, angels came to their aid and threw the Saracens into confusion. Some were slain and others captured. The prisoners were astonished to find themselves in the hands of only six men, who had taken no part in the fight. They asked what had become of the army they had encountered. The knights, who had not seen the angels themselves, then understood that they had received heavenly aid, and they responded, "When we have need they come to our aid; when we no longer need them they return to their tents."

For first-hand accounts of experience with angels we must turn to the writings of the true mystics and visionaries. One of the most noted of these was Saint Hildegarde of Bingen, who founded the Benedictine convent at Mount Saint Rupert. Hildegarde was no recluse but a remarkably able and active woman, who as abbess of a convent combined the usually inconsistent roles of seer and woman of practical affairs. Born in 1098, she was the youngest of ten children of a German knight and was consecrated by her parents to the service of God as a tithe offering. Her visions began when she was five years old and continued throughout her long life. She seems to have accepted her involuntary dedication without protest, as a royal child accepts his position in the secular world, so that the often terrifying visions and the voices she heard were never interpreted in terms of her personal life. She explained that they were not perceived by her bodily senses but seen and heard with the eyes and ears of the spirit. Brilliant lights and thunderous voices, figures of colossal size, and forms as fantastic as those Ezekiel saw, were perceived from her earliest years, and she accepted them as direct messages from God, relating wholly to the spiritual life.

Hildegarde wrote several books describing her visions with interpretations of them, which she felt had come to her from the same source as the visions themselves. Since these interpretations fitted completely within the framework of her Christian nurture, their meaning has lost much of its power for our own day, but there is no doubt of the sincerity of her account of the mystical experience, which filled her with awe and exaltation.

Angels took a prominent part in the visions, one series of which contains a complete picture of the nine orders of celestial beings. The names of the ranks follow those of the Pseudo-Dionysius the Areopagite, but the arrangement of them and the visual details are her own. Hildegarde's description of the ranks within ranks seems confusing as it progresses, but in the end an orderly pattern appears, consisting of a series of concentric circles, with the angels and archangels on the outside and the cherubim and seraphim at the center. Her archangels are not confined to four or even seven, but form a rank, unnumbered, as are the angels. The angels forming the outer rank "expand the desires of a profound intellect like wings." The archangels, consisting wholly of light, know the mysteries of God, so no form is discernible. According to the voice of God which she heard, the five battalions within the outer circles meant that "the body and soul of man, comprehending the five senses of man, ought to guide them, purified by the five wounds of My Son, to the right understanding of interior commands."

At the center of this vast circular symbol of the spiritual life, the cherubim, signifying the knowledge of God, enclose the highest rank of celestial beings, the seraphim. These, with their many wings, denote "all the distinguished orders of ecclesiastical institutions." As they "burn with the love of God, . . . so also [do] the dignitaries, secular as well as spiritual, who live with much purity in ecclesiastical mysteries." Finally, since the Church is for all men, Hildegarde included under the fiery symbol of the many-winged seraphim "all those loving souls who seek eternal life in the sincerity of a pure heart." [5] That the seraphim, the highest order in the heavenly hierarchy and the one closest to the divine center, were seen by Hildegarde in terms of the Church demonstrates the monastic spirit that dominated her life. She was never canonized, but she was so revered that she came to be accorded the title of saint and is so named in the great collection of the lives of the saints known as *Acta Sanctorum*. Although she is usually referred to as one of the great mystics, her spiritual experience belongs rather to the prophetic than the mystical type. God and man remained wholly separated in her spiritual world. She did not describe a soul's union with God, nor was she transported to heaven, as the Jewish mystics had felt they had been. Even in the ecstasies and the terrors of her visions, her German feet remained firmly on the ground, the angels showed themselves in a formal pattern before her inner sight, and the great light and thunderous voice revealed truths which were immediately applicable to life on earth.

A mystic of a wholly different type of mind was born in Germany about eighty years after the death of the Abbess Hildegarde. Johannes Eckhart entered the Dominican order at the age of fourteen and spent his most impressionable years at Cologne, where he had his training in the theological school founded a generation earlier by Thomas Aquinas. His thinking was greatly influenced by the great scholar, whom he was to succeed at Paris as champion of the Dominicans in the continuing dispute with the Franciscans. Although he returned later to Cologne as a professor, Eckhart was not to be known to posterity so much for his scholarship as for his power as a preacher. At a time when doctrine was hotly disputed by ecclesiastics but guardedly handed out to the laity in the form of imagery into which their beliefs could be projected, Eckhart preached to the common people, basing his message on his personal religious experience. Although he never denied the accepted dogmas of the Church, he cut through the crust of accumulated tradition and found his own way of interpreting the essential experience of man's relation to God.

To Meister Eckhart, all things existed only in God, and God existed in man, in the center of the soul which he called "the spark." The Trinity represented the three ways in which the unknowable Godhead manifests itself in relation to man. The Son, as the Word, is eternally being created in the soul of man, and through him the unity with God sought by the soul may be realized. The mystic birth of the Son in the soul is the central theme of Eckhart's preaching.

It is not strange that he was often misunderstood, was criticized by his own followers for expressing his views before the common people, and was finally called to account by the Inquisition at Cologne. His defense, one of the few authentic documents from his hand, is a moving revelation of the mind of a dedicated man who dared to place his fresh religious experience above the learning he shared with those who opposed him. "I may err," he said, "but I may not be a heretic, for the first has to do with the mind and the second with the will." Eckhart appealed his case to the Pope, but he did not live to hear the reply that came from Rome, condemning some of his proposals. So little is known of his life that we cannot tell whether it was shortened by the ordeal of his trial. The Pope (John XXII) declared after Eckhart's death that he had been deceived "by the father of lies, who often appears as an angel of light," and several centuries were to pass before the value of his contribution to the understanding of man's inner life was to be acknowledged.

Hildegarde of Bingen saw visions of all the angelic hosts in the glory of heaven; Thomas Aquinas devoted himself to metaphysical studies regarding their nature; but Meister Eckhart, who died in disrepute among the churchmen, conceived of them in their ancient role as ministers and messengers of God. In one of his sermons he speaks of sudden illumination through the appearance of an angel as a rare occurrence, but he suggests that the light of God, which would be too strong for the soul to bear, can be perceived through the less intense light of the angels. "Behold, I send my angel to refine the soul and prepare her for divine light." [6]

In another sermon he says, "When the Lord sends his angel to the soul she becomes sure knowing." He does not explain in what form or how the angel enters into relation with the soul; it is a psychic experience he is describing. Using as his text the exclamation of Peter when he found himself free to leave his prison, "Now I know of a surety that the Lord hath sent His angel," he reverses the sentence and says, "The Lord hath sent His angel, therefore I know of a surety," Peter, he says, stands for intuition, which penetrates ahead of knowledge, but the angel is the means by which God bestows knowledge. The soul is capable of knowing all things and she never rests until she attains her original form in which all things are one; it is there she rests in God.

Meister Eckhart's definition of an angel varies in different discourses, for he quotes as his sources the statements of several of the Church Fathers, each of whom has his own way of expressing his belief. He seems unconcerned about matters of form and substance, and confines his attention to the functions of the angels in the lives of men. The soul itself, in which the angel acts, seems to need no definition in his mind, and he assumes that his hearers are well aware of what the soul is. He repeats, however, the words of Saint Jerome and other authorities regarding the opposites in man: "Every man, because he is a man, has within him a good spirit, an angel, and also an evil spirit, a devil." But aside from naming the good and evil forces inherent in man, he seems much less concerned than his contemporaries with the warfare of the soul. His attention is fixed on the attainment of unity, and the medieval obsession with Satan as the figure to whom all evil was projected apparently was alien to his nature. His sermons contain little imagery, except as the idea of the angel itself is an image of psychic reality. The word "light" appears repeatedly to express the experience of the soul in relation to God. Light and the angels become almost synonymous in some passages where he wants to make clear the inadequacy of the intellect for understanding the spiritual realm.

> It is the function and craft of the moon and sun to give light and they do it swiftly. When they emit their rays, all the ends of the world are filled with light in a moment. Higher than these are the angels, who work with fewer instruments and also with fewer ideas. The highest seraph has only one. He comprehends as unity all that his inferiors see as manifold. But God needs no idea at all, nor has he any. He acts in the soul without instruments, idea, or likeness. He acts in the core of the soul which no idea ever penetrated—but He alone—his own essence. No creature can do this.

In another attempt to express the ineffable, however, he uses the word "idea" in almost an opposite sense:

> The authorities teach that next to the first emanation, which is the Son coming out of the Father, the angels are most like God. And it may well be true, for the soul at its highest is found like God, but an angel gives a closer idea of Him. That is all an angel is: an idea of God.

Since the order in which Meister Eckhart's sermons were given is very uncertain, it is dangerous to try to trace the development of his thought, but much of what he said concerning the place of angels in the spiritual world is summed up in the following passage:

> As regards the angels. The angels, of whatever rank, abet and assist at God's birth in the soul; that is to say, they have satisfaction, they delight and rejoice in this birth. Nothing is wrought by the angels: the birth is due to God alone and anything that ministers thereto is work of service. May God be born in us, so help us, God.
>
> Amen.

9 / THE CHANGING IMAGE

A myriad angels moved in festive play,
In brilliance and in art diversified.
—DANTE

It is disconcerting to discover that the representations from which most of us have derived our impression of how angels would look if they had bodies were made at a time when the importance of the angel in the scheme of the cosmos was already on the decline. The painters of the late Middle Ages and the Renaissance provided the Western world with thousands of angel figures, lavishing their skill on forms of esthetic beauty and often of sensitive spiritual feeling. There was an immense variety among them in design and detail, for not only did one artist's vision differ from that of another, but the place and the time brought forth certain types, so that angels of the fourteenth century can be distinguished at a glance from those of the sixteenth, and Flemish angels from those of Italy. It does not matter much in which school you trace the development of the painting of angels, for changes of a similar kind occurred in all of them. Even when the artist's themes are drawn from his religious heritage, he sees them in the atmosphere of his own time.

Once the pattern was set in the early centuries of the Christian era, the main characteristics of the angel remained constant through the first millennium. The dignity of bearing, the great feathered wings, the flowing robes or regal apparel and the aura of light represented by the nimbus impressed themselves so firmly on men's minds that they accepted them as reality rather than as symbols used to delineate a spiritual being. The manuscript painting that developed in the security of the monasteries in the time of Charlemagne and the succeeding centuries brought in a new manner but kept alive the traditional forms. The artist monks in those strongholds of the faith, many of which were remote from the older religious centers, poured new life into their creations with freer drawing and more subtle coloring than had been used earlier. Northern Europe contributed the decorative style in borders and initials that gave such grace and brilliance to the later medieval manuscripts. There is a liveliness in the manuscript paintings of the ninth and tenth centuries that foreshadowed the vigor of the stone carvings of the eleventh and twelfth. Both angels and demons abound, and some of the English manuscripts, especially, show angels taking active part in the events portrayed. In the scene of Christ's baptism, as shown in a manuscript from Winchester, four angels and a dove hover over the Lord's head. The two angels nearest to him as he stands in the water hold towels in readiness, while two others standing on the shore carry his clothes.

It was chiefly the lords and prelates who were able to enjoy such works of art. For the common people it was only in the churches that art came close to their lives. When relatively stable times brought about the building of many churches, new architectural forms developed and old ones were given new character, varying in arrangement and detail according to regional influences. The people themselves, whether laymen or monks, seem to have taken their lives with them into the Romanesque churches of France and Germany. Within the solidly constructed buildings, whose massive pillars and rounded arches bring the might of God down to earth, humanity impressed itself with such lively force upon the rigid stone that old themes appear in new guises.

If the subjects were in the main drawn from tradition, the vigor and fertility of imagination shown in the execution reflect the extraordinary vitality of the time. Eastern art had used symbolic forms of plants and animals for decorative purposes, but the Romanesque stone carvers gave them a life of their own. The capitals of columns burgeoned with living creatures, human as well as animal. People are seen at work, in war, and in worship. At Autun a Crusader and a pilgrim on horseback represent the contemporary scene. At Oloron Sainte Marie a pair of Moorish captives support a column on the façade, while at Anzy le Duc we find acrobats and wrestlers, whose presence may be accounted for by the symbolism of the struggles of the soul. Although evil spirits could not enter the church, lively images of them in many forms appear in the sanctuaries from which they were excluded. Satan himself appears frequently in his role of tempter as well as the ruler of

Hell. In the scene of the temptation of Jesus he is some-times shown with a covering of long hair like that of a shaggy beast, such as Dante described a couple of centuries later.

In the Romanesque carvings there seems to be no distinc-tion between inner and outer experience—between natural and supernatural, or physical and spiritual. Life is continu-ous and all of one substance. The angels hold their earlier places in heaven but share the general vitality and appear in particular activities. A penitent, rising from his knees, might look up and see far above him the figures of an angel and a demon in energetic combat, and he would be com-forted, knowing that he was not alone in his struggle against evil. The angels were fighting for him.

Over the portal of almost every church, Christ sits en-throned, surrounded by angels, saints, and apostles, and often by the symbolic figures of the four Evangelists. In spite of the orderly use of space in the whole architectural design, each figure is distinct and individual. The angels forming an arch above the head of the Lord, even within their restricted limits, are all in motion, flying, turning, dancing, descending head first from a cloud, or striding forward in balance between heaven and earth. They are not mere attendants at the heavenly court, but integral parts of the universal whole, in which life in heaven and life on earth are equally meaningful constituents.

Since cultural changes occur imperceptibly, there is no distinct end to one period and no definite beginning to an-other, though the building of the cathedral at Chartres is generally seen as a turning-point between the Romanesque and the Gothic styles. Under the stimulation of the great intellectual awakening of the twelfth century, light began to stream into the churches as well as into men's minds, and a new sense of order modified and shaped earlier styles into more disciplined forms. In spite of this general tendency, Gothic forms remained immensely varied, so that we find no prevailing type in the representation of angels. Some have wings, some have not; some take the restricted shapes that are most consistent with the special architectural features of which they form a part, while others still appear in the free movement characteristic of the Romanesque. Demons still held their place in architecture as in life, and were even pictured in more loathsome forms than before. Satan still walked the earth, claiming his rights in the souls of men.

The court of heaven also kept its ancient grandeur in the cosmic picture officially sanctioned by the Church and generally accepted by the people. Dante, standing like a bridge between the Middle Ages and the Renaissance, saw angels of majestic bearing engaged in their duties as guards and guides of the human spirits that entered the other world. At the beginning of the *Purgatorio* he describes the coming of a boat in which the spirits are brought over the sea to the shores of Purgatory, with an angel at the helm. The angel's wings are stretched up toward heaven to act as sails, and the light that surrounds him is so intense that Dante is unable to look at it.

> Such an exceeding brightness did allume
> The Bird of God, who near and nearer bore,
> Mine eyes to endure him might not now presume.

To Dante, as to Meister Eckhart, the quality of the angel is best expressed in terms of light, but in Dante's poem we find foreshadowed the different view of the angel's function that brought about the gradual change in form to be seen in religious paintings after the thirteenth century. It is in the *Paradiso* that we find the clue to the nature of this change.

When at last the poet, having completed the journey up the seven-story mountain of Purgatory, parts from Virgil, who cannot accompany him in Paradise, he joins Beatrice and sees for himself the order of the celestial spheres. Here it is again light that seems to move him most strongly. The nine ranks of angels in their concentric circles move around a central point of light

> of so intense a beam
> That needs must every eye it blazes on
> Be closed before its poignancy extreme.

When they leave the Primum Mobile and enter heaven itself, Dante finds it a realm of pure light. He likens it to a radiant white rose, in which the angels flit in and out like bees.

> Their faces all were as a flame intense
> Their wings of gold, the rest so pure a white
> That never snow could dazzle so the sense.

In this dwelling place of the redeemed spirits are the saints, and it is here that Beatrice has to leave Dante to take her appointed place. Since a new guide is needed, one would expect to find that an angel, perhaps even the guardian of the Church, the archangel Michael, would be assigned to accompany him. A modern reader is likely to feel a little disappointment as, nearing the climax of the ecstatic vision, he finds himself instead in the company of that great and fiery preacher, Bernard of Clairvaux. With Saint Bernard as his final guide, Dante is granted a vision of the Queen of Heaven, the Virgin Mary, on her throne, surrounded by angels, whom he describes as "the sacred minds . . . created through the heavenly height to fly." Beside her stands Gabriel, the archangel of the Annunciation, looking into her eyes with such love that "he seems one flame of living light." Saint Bernard's prayer to her in behalf of the poet is answered by a momentary glimpse into the divine mystery within the Eternal Light, which he finds beyond the power of words to describe. He concludes the poem:

> To the high imagination force now failed;
> But like to a wheel whose circling nothing jars
> Already on my desire and will prevailed
> The Love that moves the sun and the other stars.[1]

To people of Dante's own time, early in the fourteenth century, it would have seemed entirely appropriate to choose Saint Bernard as guide and interpreter in the final scene of this great adventure of the imagination. It was he who had fought with ardent fanaticism nearly two centuries earlier on the side of faith and love against the new intellectualism emanating from Paris. Reliance on reason in matters of religion seemed to him dangerous and un-Christian, though it would probably be an oversimplification to reduce the great dispute to a matter of heart versus head. Bernard's way prevailed over Abelard's at the time and was followed by the majority of Christians in succeeding generations. The essence of his teaching may not have been grasped by the people, but certain points of emphasis found a response in the spirit of the time. It is to Bernard we must give credit for the intensification of the cult of the Virgin Mary that began in the later Middle Ages. He taught nothing that had not previously been embodied in the doctrines of the Church, but with the authority of an inspired preacher he promoted certain new attitudes that strongly influenced the practices of a later time. It was he who fostered the worship of the Virgin as mediatrix through his statement "God willed that we have nothing that does not pass through Mary's hands." A century later Saint Anthony of Padua was to add another degree to her high estate when he saw her as co-redemptrix with her son.

As the Christian world expanded and secular life became more complicated, heaven began to seem immeasurably remote. Humanity closed in upon itself and found new values in the here and now. For the rank and file of the Virgin Mary's adorers it was her closeness rather than her position in a theological system that endeared her to them. She was the Great Mother, the all-loving giver to whom they could turn for help even while she remained on her throne in the now distant heaven. There the angels were depicted as her attendants, hovering behind her throne or showing their adoration as Gabriel did in Dante's final scene. If they were "sacred minds" and pure "intelligences," wholly immaterial, as Thomas Aquinas declared them, they could not be persons, whereas the Mother of God had been a living woman and kept her feminine characteristics even as Queen of Heaven. She made herself known through visions granted to devout persons and through many miracles that occurred at her shrines. Those with guilty consciences laid their burdens at her feet, for a mother will always understand and forgive.

There had always been a Great Mother in religions from the time when the miracle of fertility in the earth itself was worshiped in primitive forms. In the strictly masculine monotheism of the Hebrews, however, the cult of the maternal principle was prohibited. Neighboring tribes all practiced it, and the Hebrew prophets were constantly inveighing against those of their own people who had gone astray and worshiped at the shrines of Ashteroth. It was not until the time of the Cabalists of southern France and Spain in the twelfth and thirteenth centuries that Jewish mystics gave recognition to the feminine element when they defined the image of God as a unity made up of ten potencies, male and female. After the coming of Christianity in the gentile lands of the eastern Mediterranean, a new outlet was found in Mary, the mother of the Christ, for the feminine element that had been represented in the old religions by the female deities. In the West, the cult was of much slower growth. Some early authorities placed the archangels above Mary in the hierarchy of heaven.

What combination of circumstances, historical or psychological, brought the cult of Mary into full flower during the Middle Ages would be hard to state, but the growth of her popularity is not the only evidence that the feminine principle was given new recognition at that time. In another form it appeared in the contemporary ideals of chivalry with its highly organized code of behavior. If Bernard was the promoter of the cult of the Virgin Mary, the man whom he implacably opposed, Abelard, also made his contribution to the trend of the time with his outspoken claim for the values represented by womanhood. In the monastic world the only women to be honored were the

dedicated virgins or those who had rejected their femininity. According to Abelard, man was to see his ideals in
woman, and passionate love was to be encouraged. Abelard
not only loved one woman, but understood that man finds
his own soul reflected in the feminine image.

Behind all the violence of the late Middle Ages, the striving for power, religious and secular, and the strange mix-
ture of aspiration, zeal, and hate that had marked the era of
the Crusades, this new theme had been weaving its way
into the pattern of the times. Abelard may have been an
agent of it rather than an instigator when he declared his
faith in feminine values in the spiritual life. One aspect of
the new ideal was the growth of romantic love. Having
first found its expression in the age of the troubadours, it
survived the gradual decay of chivalry and won a place in
European life from which it was never entirely dislodged.
The idealization of woman on one hand and the fear of her
power in a manmade world on the other created a double-
faced image, half angel, half demon. In some instances a
woman was seen as wholly demonic. The figure of the
witch took much of the blame for the forces of evil over
several centuries.

Meanwhile, the Christian Church had been accumulating
a vast number of saints. Every time and every locality had
produced its holy ones, both men and women, whose acts
of piety and mercy had given them fame. Their miracles
while on earth had become legendary, and it was natural to
suppose that their souls in heaven could use the same
powers. They, like Mary, had once been human, and now
in Paradise they might be thought of as her courtiers, just
as the angels were her attendants. Their lives on earth had

brought them close to the divine, but in heaven they were still concerned with affairs on earth and could mediate for humanity in cases appropriate to their particular virtues. The early Church had encouraged reverence for the martyrs, but worship of them had not been permitted. It was the desire of the people rather than the teaching of the Church that developed the cult of the saints. They took the place of the angels as links between heaven and earth.

It must have been in the time when saints took precedence over angels that the archangel Michael was given the title "Saint." Since by derivation the word "saint" merely implies holiness, it could be appropriately used for any of the celestial beings, but by association it has always been applied to the sanctified souls of men and women. In the early days of the Church all its members were called saints. When the prince of heaven was given the title, he was brought closer to humanity—perhaps as testimony to his popularity. The fact that it was Michael who, according to the Book of Revelation, had cast Satan out of heaven at the time of the Fall doubtless made him the most powerful ally in the continual battle against the devil on earth. He was no longer thought of as the weigher and judge of souls; his militant characteristics particularly endeared him to the medieval world. It is ironical that this chief of the princes of heaven, appointed far in the past to be the protector of Israel, presided over the Church throughout the persecutions of the Jews that began in the thirteenth century. By this time the other archangels, Gabriel and Raphael, who in modern times are also sometimes given the title "Saint," had receded into their historical niches, and Uriel was seldom mentioned.

Michael alone remained in close relation to the times. At
the beginning of the book *Mont Saint Michel and Chartres*,
Henry Adams gives a clear picture of the position of Saint
Michael in the medieval world.

> The Archangel loved heights. Standing on the summit
> of the tower that crowned his church, wings upspread,
> sword uplifted, the devil crawling beneath, and the cock,
> symbol of eternal vigilance, perched on his mailed foot,
> Saint Michael held a place of his own in heaven and on
> earth, which seems, in the eleventh century, to leave
> hardly room for the Virgin in the crypt at Chartres, still
> less for the Beau Christ of the thirteenth century at Am-
> iens. The Archangel stands for Church and State, and both
> militant. He is the conqueror of Satan, the mightiest of all
> created spirits, the nearest to God.[2]

Adams was writing of the eleventh century, but four
centuries later Michael's paramount position was still firm,
though he was seen less as an archangel than as the mighti-
est of the saints.

It is natural that Joan of Arc should have had a vision of
the warrior archangel. According to her own account, she
had at first only heard voices, but after she had become accustomed to hearing them she began to see the speakers,
Saint Michael, Saint Catherine, and Saint Margaret, who always came in a cloud of heavenly light. She knew it was
Saint Michael because he spoke "with the tongue of
angels." Perhaps the reason her visions made so strong an
impression on the people of her own time was that tales of
such manifestations were becoming increasingly rare. Most
of the great mystics of the fourteenth century, not long
past, had sought a more direct relation with the divine

source, and received their revelations through an inner experience.

One of these, the English anchoress called the Lady Julian, who lived out her long life in a little house attached to the wall of the parish church of Saint Julian at Conisford, recorded a remarkable series of revelations that came to her at the crisis of an illness in 1373, when she was thirty years old. Not expecting to live, she desired to experience the passion of Christ, and it was at this point the sixteen revelations began, coming in close succession. In her book, called *Revelations of Divine Love*,[3] they are clearly separated, having to do with such themes as the Trinity, the passion of Christ, the oneness of God and man, God's mercy and grace, man's travail against sin, and the indwelling of God in the soul. She saw no angels and heard no voices from heaven, for all these revelations were inwardly experienced. She felt that they were given, but that they came through her own mental perceptions, which were wide open to receive them.

It was only when the force of evil thrust its way in that the Lady Julian saw anything concrete, and then it came in the form of a dream. She described in detail the horrible appearance of the fiend who caught her by the throat and would have strangled her had she not held fast to her trust in God. Her encounter with the personification of evil followed the revelations of love, as if it were a trial to test her faith or a necessary reaction from sublimity too great for a mortal to carry back into life. Neither of these explanations, however, seems to have been her own. She did not consider the attacks of the evil one part of the revelations but an interference from an outside force. Men and women

[135

had not yet acknowledged the devil in themselves, but still saw him as an objective reality to be met on the level of earthly existence.

If Satan still plagued the faithful with his terrifying power, the existence of the angels of light could hardly have been doubted by any but the few who rejected the way of religion altogether. They had simply become obscured by the greater glory of the Holy Mother and the more direct appeal of the saints. But there was still another reason for their retirement. The Lady Julian, like her contemporary, the anonymous author of *The Cloud of Unknowing*,[4] represented a trend that was preparing the way for the Reformation. The desire she felt to share the passion of Christ found another voice half a century later in one of the most widely read books in Christendom, the *Imitatio Christi*. Thomas a Kempis, to whom it is attributed, was not born until after the Lady Julian received her revelations, but he carried further the view that the inner transformation of the soul was to be accomplished through following the pattern laid down by Jesus Christ in his life as man, rather than through the sacraments and other observances. This was one of the movements of the time, which, though having little effect on the masses, were part of the process of the humanization of values that brought about the Renaissance.

No one could claim that an anchoress in England or a monk in Germany, or any other individual, had a direct or even a remote influence on the representation of angels in art. It is simply that all of these trends were signs of the times, and that artists generally reflect the feeling of the period in which they live. If the great painters of the fifteenth century caught the mood of their own time, it is clear that angels not only had become mere adjuncts to the main theme, but that the concept of angelic nature had undergone a drastic change.

The Byzantine angels had the faces and figures of young men, but they had the bearing of persons of authority. The impression they gave was of agelessness. Romanesque angels, having thrown off the static quality of the Byzantine image, had the liveliness of youth, though the faces, sometimes strongly masculine, sometimes verging on the feminine, still seemed sufficiently removed from humanity to escape the question of age. In scenes like that of the Last Judgment, where the purpose was to give an effect of great solemnity, they still retained their ancient dignity. But in the Gothic period, with all its variety in form and type and costume, the general tendency was toward representing angels as innocent adolescents, while still preserving, in most instances, a spiritual quality. The smiling angel first appeared in France in the thirteenth century, and in the fourteenth century angel children could be seen in both France and Germany. They are not found in Italian painting for another century. The angels of Giotto and Duccio, early in the fourteenth century, have strong, solemn faces, and their figures, even in free movement, are mature and dignified. Remnants of the Byzantine convention, which continued without interruption in the East, still clung to the painting of Italy.

According to Christian tradition, angels are sexless beings, in spite of the verse in Genesis that tells how the sons of God took wives of the daughters of men—a passage, as we have seen, that some Jewish writers had associated with the angels who fell from heaven. Yet no one before the nineteenth century would have thought of speaking of an angel as "she." The characteristics of angels as seen before the thirteenth century would have weighed heavily on the masculine side. The central place of the Madonna and Child in the art of the three ensuing centuries seems to have caused them to shed a light of femininity on all around them. Angels became more fragile, more gentle, more endearing, as they hovered around the throne. They were often smaller than the principal figures, since they were of less importance. They played musical instruments and offered playthings to the Holy Child. In any of the scenes from the life of Christ they might be found soaring in the sky like small blue or red birds, with their feet tucked inside trailing robes. The nimbus of Byzantine tradition appeared less often around their heads, but certain conventions in dress and arrangement of hair were still observed.

There were always exceptions, of course, and an occasional angel figure even in the sixteenth century expressed majesty. Fra Angelico, who so lovingly created a garden of Paradise for the souls of the blessed, held a middle position between two periods. The grace of his angel figures and their young faces with carefully curled hair were of his own time, but he used the solid gold nimbus and maintained the dignity of the earlier tradition. Later a single circle of light floated above the heads of the angels of Florentine painters such as Botticelli. Finally it was abandoned altogether as the figures became ever more youthful and more human, while the costume and the arrangement of hair changed to fit the new aspect. The Flemish painters, who lived in a cold climate, were apt to dress their demure, oval-faced angels in heavy embroidered cloaks of ecclesiastical pattern.

Where the archangels were concerned, something of the manly character was usually preserved, especially in the case of Michael, who, even with the face of a youth too young to bear arms, appeared most often in complete armor. Gabriel, who had been chiefly represented in the scene of the Annunciation, began to be seen with the horn with which he was to announce the Last Judgment. In this role he shows his old fire, whereas in the other he had become less the representative of Deity than an adorer of the Virgin, to whom he did obeisance. Raphael, whom Milton was later to call "the affable Archangel," was charming but almost wholly feminine as he walked beside Tobias on the long journey they took together.

By the sixteenth century angel children had become so human that unless they showed their wings they were hardly distinguishable from mortals. As long as they were clothed they maintained a certain propriety as they played at the feet of the Mother and Child, but in the sky, where they were draped in a bit of gauze or more often were nude, they tumbled over one another with the exuberance of a litter of puppies. Sometimes their infant bodies seemed to be merged with the clouds to form a background for the divine figures, or even a platform under their feet.

A similar transformation had overtaken the cherubim, members of the highest rank in the celestial hierarchy. Ezekiel's visions may never have been read by the artists or their sponsors, since the Bible was seldom in the hands of laymen during the Middle Ages. His enigmatic figures had in the course of time been pulled apart, and their symbolism used in other connections. We have seen that since early Christian times the four faces had been interpreted as symbols of the four Evangelists, as such becoming entirely separated from the six wings and the wheels of the original figure. Italian painters sometimes used the wings alone to cover and surround the figure of the Savior on the cross. By the fifteenth century the cherubim themselves had been reduced to infantile heads with one pair or sometimes two pairs of wings, forming a sort of rosette which was very decorative in borders but had nothing to do with the Biblical conception.

Authority was now altogether missing from the angel image. Innocence, sweetness, grace, and joyousness, all characteristics of youth, gave pleasure to the eye and such relief to the soul as the companionship of amiable children can provide. It is true that certain ideas persisted in regard to the ministry of the angels, but the sense of awe was missing and revelations were rare. Human children were taught that each person had his special guardian who was with him at all times, and devout souls nearing death hoped for the approach of the angels to ease them gently upward when the time came for them to climb "the steep ascent of heaven."

Christian art had long since lost its purpose as a means of instruction for the people. In the sixteenth century it merged with the broadening stream of esthetic expression that flowed from the newly revived sources of antiquity on one side and on the other from the new discoveries that were taking place, not only in the physical world but in the world of thought. The infant angels with their quick responses and their joyous movements may have been a true representation of the spirit of the time. The medieval pattern had come to an end, and the world was teeming with new ideas.

10 / DIVERSITY OF VIEWS

The sound of glory ringing in our ears;
Without, our shame; within, our consciences;
Angels and grace, eternal hopes and fears.
— GEORGE HERBERT

While the cherubs of Western Europe were disporting themselves among the clouds, monks of the Greek Orthodox Church were still copying manuscripts and painting Byzantine angels on the domes of their churches. It is ironic that the ecclesiastical art of the Eastern Church should have remained static during the time when the spread of Eastern culture westward after the fall of Constantinople was a vital influence in the development of Western thought.

In 1855 a German scholar translated into his own language a manuscript he had found in use in a monastery on the isolated craggy peninsula of Mount Athos.[1] It was a fifteenth-century handbook for painters, giving detailed directions for the decoration of churches according to the old tradition. It is supposed to have been written by one

Dionysius of Fourna for the use of the monks who dedicated themselves to religious art. When the translator, G. Schafer, visited Mount Athos it was still considered authoritative, and a hundred years later another visitor found some of the monks still painting holy pictures according to the same prescriptions. Although there have certainly been modifications of style in places less cut off from the world, Eastern ecclesiastical art in general still appears as the direct descendant of the early Byzantine, in contrast to that of the West, which has reflected the changes in the secular world around it.

According to the handbook, each subject was to be treated according to a fixed formula, and the divine figures, saints, prophets, and angels were to be shown in characteristic poses. Each rank of angels was represented in its own special colors, with prescribed costumes and attributes. The lowest order, for instance, the princedoms, archangels, and angels, who were closest to man, wore armor with gold girdles and carried axes and spears. The symbols of the four Evangelists were combined in a conventionalized figure called the Tetramorph, which consisted of the six wings of the seraphim with an angel's head surrounded by a nimbus, above which appears the eagle, while to the right side is a lion and to the left a calf.

The care given to the right representation of the celestial figures is in accord with the prominent place held by the angels in the Eastern Orthodox Churches. In a litany still in use, the priest says to the people, "For an angel of peace, a faithful guide, a guardian of our souls and bodies, let us entreat the Lord." Some of the prayers are addressed directly to the angels. A liturgy for November 8, the feast of Saint

Michael and Saint Gabriel, contains this hymn of dismissal: "O Leaders of the Heavenly Host, unworthy as we are, we implore you that by your prayers you will encircle us with the protection of your wings of unseen glory; guard us who bend low before you and fervently cry; release us from dangers, O Marshals of the Powers above."

In the Roman Church it was not until 1608 that a feast in honor of guardian angels was established, and then it was by particular request of local churches, at the desire of the people. The question arises why the cry for the recognition of guardian angels should be heard at the time when the penetration of humanistic ideas and the birth of modern scientific thinking were rapidly changing the intellectual atmosphere. Some scholars suggest that it was encouraged by the clergy because the cult of saints had grown out of hand. By that time Luther and Calvin had lived and died, had uttered their protests and found ready audiences. They had cracked open the solidarity of the Church, leaving behind them a new dynamic force that sprang from the many honest souls that were moved to contrition and found renewal. On the other side, Ignatius Loyola had founded the Society of Jesus and had become a leader of the Counter-Reformation, spreading the Gospel to all parts of the expanding world. Wealth had poured into Europe from other continents, strides had been taken toward more general education, literature and the arts were flourishing. But some people still felt the need of a personal tie between themselves and the heaven that had been so far removed by the push of physical expansion and by man's increasing consciousness of himself.

It is a curious fact that the first such call for the recognition on the church calendar of guardian angels came from Cordova in Spain, from which the Jews, to whom guardian angels were important, had been expelled at the end of the preceding century. This was probably a mere coincidence, yet who would dare to say that the intricate workings of men's minds are not affected by such events? It has happened more than once that "the stone which the builders rejected is become the head of the corner." Cordova, a seat of Moorish power, had had a strong Jewish colony, and the Jewish philosopher Maimonides, whose writings were of great interest to Christian scholars in the Middle Ages, was born there.

Some of the exiled Jews, meanwhile, after suffering the misfortunes of the dispossessed, had established a center in Palestine, where in the sixteenth century a group of rabbis followed the mystical way explored by the Cabalists and left records of their experiences. The guardian angel of Jewish tradition became for these seekers an attendant spirit, whom they could summon through the exercise of certain disciplines and through whom they could receive revelations of divine truth. One of these mystics, Joseph Karo, a well-known author of books of rabbinic orthodoxy, kept a diary in which he recorded his experiences with his spirit, who was known as a *maggid*.[2] Through the diligent study of the Law and the performance of the divine commandments, a new angel was created who became the revealer of truth to the individual who had brought him into being. The divine commandments must be perfectly performed, or the corresponding maggid would be imperfect and composed of good and evil. The mystic, thoroughly trained in the Law and the scriptures, was careful to distinguish between the vagaries of his own personality and the inspired message, which he felt must conform to the sacred texts even though it might contain a new truth. Karo's maggid was neither identical with the Greek daemon nor with the Jewish guardian angel, but was considered a manifestation of Shekinah, the male-female earthly presence of God. He stood at the highest reach of the human spirit and could be apprehended only by a person of pure motives. Without this standard, Jewish mysticism often drifted off into the realm of magic. To call an angel's name was to summon him, and an angel could be very helpful in pursuing one's personal concerns.

Since opposites are always present in human developments, the spirit of inquiry characteristic of the age was coupled with a general preoccupation with the occult in Jewish and Christian circles alike. The dissemination of ideas through printed books brought before a wider public subjects that had hitherto been left to the few. Books abounded, not only on such disciplined practices as astrology and alchemy, in which lay hidden a fund of ancient wisdom concerning the soul of man, but on a variety of manifestations of the spirit world such as demons, witches, and familiar spirits.

Martin Luther, that stalwart protagonist of the life of faith based on the word of God as revealed in the Bible, had not wanted to see angels or to hear their voices. This was not a matter of disbelief; he never denied that angels existed, and he spoke of them as "the Lord's soldiers, guardians, leaders, and protectors to preserve the creatures which He had created." In spite of this view of the functions of angels as centered in the life of man rather than as

Duccio, "The Temptation of Christ," 1311, (Photo: Copyright 1965 by The Frick Collection, New York)

Giotto, "The Lamentation," 1305–1306, fresco from the Arena Chapel, Padua. (Photo: Alinari)

Masolino (1384–c.1435), "The Annunciation." (National Gallery of
Art, Washington, D.C.; Andrew Mellon Collection)

Hans Memling (1430?–1494), "Madonna and Child with Angels." (National Gallery of Art, Washington, D.C.; Andrew Mellon Collection)

El Greco (1541–1614), "The Virgin with Saints Ines and Tecla." (National Gallery of Art, Washington, D.C.; Widener Collection)

"Satan with His Angels Lying on the Burning Lake," from the first illustrated edition of *Paradise Lost*, 1688 (fourth edition). (Courtesy Harvard College Library, Cambridge, Mass.)

"Michael Tells Adam and Eve That They Must Leave the Garden of Eden," from the 1688 illustrated edition of *Paradise Lost*. (Courtesy Harvard College Library, Cambridge, Mass.)

"Pilgrims on the Road to Heaven," illustration from the tenth edition of *Pilgrim's Progress*, 1685. (New York Public Library)

Rembrandt, "The Annunciation," c. 1650. (Musée des Beaux Arts, Besançon; photo: Rijksmuseum, Amsterdam)

Rembrandt, "Vision of Daniel," c. 1652. (The Louvre, Paris)

members of the court of heaven, Luther entreated the Lord not to send him any visions. His reason for hoping to avoid angelic revelations was characteristic of the course he set for himself in his desire to remove all clutter from the clearly marked, though narrow, path of the Christian. All the essentials of his teaching were contained in the Ten Commandments, the Apostles' Creed, and the Lord's Prayer. In his commentary on the Book of Genesis he said:

> From the beginning of my Reformation I have asked God to send me neither dreams, nor visions, nor angels, but to give me the right understanding of His Word, the Holy Scriptures; for as long as I have God's Word, I know that I am walking in His way and that I shall not fall into any error or delusion. Had I followed the enthusiasts and their dreams and visions, I would have had to change my doctrine more than thirty or forty times.[3]

Luther's skepticism about dreams appeared a number of times in his writings. He acknowledged that the Holy Spirit had sometimes made revelations to the prophets through that medium, but the devil too, "who likes to imitate God," deceives men by causing them to dream lying dreams. Of the power of Satan he said:

> Jesus pictures him as a giant who keeps a castle. He has not only the world in possession, but he fortifies it that no human creature can take it from him. And just as a castle held by a tyrant can only be won by a stronger giant, even so mankind must be delivered and regained from the Devil by Christ.

Satan, as prince of this world, Luther said, has hosts of demons that serve under his leadership, "and they cause much

[147

confusion, harm, and wrong-doing in the home, church and state." The heathen, he says, know of the existence of evil spirits, but they do not know that God rules the world through the agency of the holy angels. Rather wistfully he adds, "Just why God thus exerts his rule, Scripture does not tell us."

In the theology of the Reformation the "prince of this world" and his demons remained as firm in their position of power as ever, and it would be a long time before Protestantism would dislodge them. When they did sink out of the Protestant consciousness, it was not so much by any doctrinal shift on the part of the governing bodies of the churches as by the slow rise of other influences. Some Protestant bodies today retain the requirement in the baptism of infants that the sponsors reject in the child's behalf "the devil and all his works," though few of those concerned would interpret the ancient wording literally.

John Calvin, whose teaching eventually became widespread and led to the establishment of numerous church bodies, maintained that Satan could not act except by the will and with the permission of God, since he was created by him. Together with his doctrine of predestination, this belief would have left the average human being in a rather hopeless position if man's natural tendency to see himself in the right had not enabled him to believe he was one of the elect. Since neither Luther nor Calvin counted on angelic help except in the most general terms, but did see "the ancient foe" as a vital and omnipresent force in the world, seeking the destruction of the soul, life again became a strenuous battlefield, as it has been for the early Christians.

The Protestants had their martyrs too, for each side of the split church saw the devil projected into the other.

The angels of light may have been thrust aside by the urgency of building a new way of life, but the image of them was not erased from the minds of men. The Bible was the word of God. There were angels in the Bible, therefore angels must be considered a part of God's plan for the universe. Since there was no longer an authoritative body whose statements could be accepted without question, everything was to be seen in a new light. The spirit of the Reformation had given each individual the responsibility for his own soul in relation to God. Freedom to think one's own thoughts inspired a spate of speculation on angels.

While Protestant philosophers and clergymen were seeking a rational place for angels in their system of thought, a Lutheran shoemaker in a small town in Germany was receiving revelations which he could not account for except as an act of divine grace. Jakob Boehme, a contemporary of Shakespeare and Galileo, was a mystic less by intention than by compulsion, for much of his writing was of an automatic nature. In describing how it happened he said, "It comes and goes as a sudden shower," and often he felt so pushed by its rapid flow that he could not take time to write correctly. Boehme was one of those who are found rather than of those who seek. In his *Confessions* he wrote:

> I never desired to know anything of the Divine Mystery, much less understood I the way to seek it. . . . I sought only after the heart of Jesus Christ, that I might hide myself therein from the wrathful anger of God and the violent assaults of the Devil. . . . In this my earnest and

Christian seeking and desire . . . the Gate was opened to
me, that in one quarter of an hour I saw and knew more
than if I had been many years together at an University.[4]

Boehme had a very limited education, but some scholars
think they see traces of his reading in similarities to the
thought of Paracelsus and other philosophers. He sometimes lacked the words to express what he saw, and occasionally he borrowed terms which failed to clarify his
meaning, but his conception of the unity of all things in a
spiritual and material whole is obviously the result of a
spontaneous vision before which he felt himself to be only
a humble observer.

Like other mystics, Boehme experienced the sensation of
being surrounded by light. The first time it came to him as
a youth, the light remained with him for seven days. Unlike most of the earlier mystics, he found the way to the
revelations led through the contemplation of nature. When
he was twenty-five, while sitting in the fields, he experienced for the first time a sudden flash of understanding in
which were revealed to him "the essence, use and proper-
ties of the grasses and herbs." This led to further revelations in regard to "the whole Creation," and to the beginning of his automatic writing.

Boehme was not aware of any angelic intervention. In
fact he said, "If an angel from heaven should tell me this
. . . I could not believe it. . . . But the Sun itself arises in
my spirit, and therefore I am most sure of it." What we
earlier described as the angel experience was in him an inner
one, and was recognized as such, but the revelations related
the inner with the outer aspects of the spiritual world.
While scientists and philosophers struggled with the intel-

lectual problem of the relation between the physical and the spiritual, Jakob Boehme simply "saw" them as one. Yes, heaven and the angels do exist, but they are not separated from the material world, he said; they interpenetrate and surround man and nature. "The holy angels converse and walk up and down in the innermost of the world." When the soul leaves the body it does not go far. "It is set in the innermost moving, and there it is with God and in God, and with all the holy angels, and can suddenly be above and suddenly beneath; it is not hindered by anything." Likewise, there is no separation between heaven and hell. "The evil and the good angels dwell near one another, and yet there is the greatest immense distance between them. For heaven is in hell and hell is in heaven, and yet the one is not manifest to the other." [5]

Since deity to Boehme is not the anthropomorphic God of most of his fellow Christians, but the underlying spiritual force from which everything in the universe springs, evil must also come from God. He identifies it with the wrathful side of God as represented in the Bible. In a chapter on Lucifer in his first book, *Aurora*, he gives an extraordinary picture of the source from which it emanates:

> The whole Deity has in its innermost or beginning Birth, in the Pith or Kernel, a very tart, terrible *Sharpness*, in which the astringent Quality is very horrible, tart, hard, dark and cold Attraction or Drawing together, like *Winter*, when there is a fierce, bitter cold Frost, when Water is frozen into Ice, and besides is very intolerable. [6]

This description reminds one of Dante's frozen hell, but to Dante the abode of Satan and the heaven of God the creator were at opposite poles.

Boehme was neither a scientist nor a theologian, and his work was not accepted by either group. His first book was privately circulated, but at Gorlitz, where he lived, it brought him under attack by a hostile pastor. He was called before the local council and forbidden to write any more. For six years he observed the order, but meanwhile he was gaining a considerable reputation as a philosopher, and when the inimical pastor moved elsewhere he felt that he was released from his enforced silence. His books were widely read by those who were willing to risk exposure to them, and some of his ideas entered the narrow stream of religious-philosophical thought that was to be explored further by later unorthodox minds. By bringing heaven and earth together again after their long separation, Boehme made a contribution of which he could not have been aware toward an understanding of the inner world of man himself. In his own life he achieved peace of soul and lived for some years after the period of his illuminations modestly and contentedly, in spite of poverty and persecutions. When he lay dying, according to an account given by his son, he heard beautiful music which was inaudible to other persons in the room.

Boehme placed his inseparable heaven and hell in close relation to the inner life of man, but the work of two writers of about his own time pictured good and evil in terms which the general public could more easily grasp. In England, Milton and Bunyan, both of the Puritan persuasion, published their wholly different books in the same year, 1667. *Paradise Lost*, Milton's cosmic drama in sonorous verse, and Bunyan's *Pilgrim's Progress*, a prose allegory of the Christian life, reflect the diverse characteristics of their creators. The first was a man of great learning and a prodigious imagination; the second was uneducated but devout, and was endowed with innate wisdom rather than a poetic mind. While Milton fought his battles for religious freedom with tracts and treatises, Bunyan was jailed for his zeal in preaching at unlawful meetings. While Milton derived many of his conceptions from Greek philosophers and found much of his imagery in classical sources, Bunyan never departed from the ideas he drew directly from the Bible, inventing his allegorical figures to fit closely the demands of his theme, the salvation of the soul.

Both authors were convinced that the Bible was the word of God, but Milton used the Biblical text only as a framework on which to build his epic. Although his theme is ostensibly the fall of man, his readers become aware that the real hero of *Paradise Lost* is Satan, a gigantic figure closely akin to that of Prometheus, who wrested power from the gods and was punished for his presumption. Milton poured into this imagined figure such vitality, intelligence, and passion that the archangels are pallid by comparison. It is Satan, shut out from heaven and claiming supreme power in hell, who speaks as a philosopher the often quoted lines

> The mind is its own place, and in itself
> Can make a Heaven of Hell, a Hell of Heaven.

Even in defeat he remains a heroic figure, his pride unvanquished and his espousal of evil a matter of his own choice.

> Farewell, remorse! All good to me is lost;
> Evil, be thou my good: by thee at least
> Divided empire with Heaven's King I hold

> By thee, and more than half perhaps will reign;
> As man ere long, and this new World shall know.[7]

In his book *Lucifer and Prometheus*, Zwi Werblowsky accounts for Milton's Satan as the product of a great mind divided between the Greek view of life and that of the Judaeo-Christian tradition. The war between heaven and hell is in a sense the conflict between Milton's conception of the value of human culture and his Puritan denial of value to everything that is of the earth. In spite of himself, and probably without intention, Milton created a character with the potential power to reconcile the opposites of good and evil. A century later William Blake was to be caught by Milton's dilemma and to carry on the idea of the value found in the dark forces within the human mind.

The more singleminded author of *The Pilgrim's Progress* saw no value in his personification of evil. Bunyan's Apollyon, named after the "angel of the abyss" in the ninth chapter of Revelation, is neither a philosopher nor a hero but a "foul fiend." When Christian encounters him straddling the road to Immanuel's Land, he uses the sword given him at the palace called Beautiful in a struggle in which he is able to wound his gigantic opponent and escape from him, only to meet evil in specific forms in the Slough of Despond, in the Giant Despair, and in characters met along the road. In his battle with Apollyon, Christian was aided by the archangel Michael, and in his gratitude said:

> Therefore to him let me give lasting praise,
> And thank and bless his holy name always.

Milton's heaven is seen as an armed camp in which the angels, under the command of Michael, engage in manly sports during their free hours and go forth to battle against the hosts of hell led by the rebellious Satan. His more gracious scenes take place in the still peaceful earthly Paradise, where Gabriel commands the night watch of the cherubim, where Uriel slides down a sunbeam to reach the earth, and Raphael shares the evening meal of Adam and Eve. Bunyan's heaven is the New Jerusalem, the home of the angels, whom he calls "the shining ones," and the bourne of the saved souls. His angels are ministering spirits who never depart from their roles as seen in the Bible. In the gold-paved streets of the heavenly city the "spirits of just men made perfect" join them in a great chorus of praise.

Since the message of *The Pilgrim's Progress* is given in pure allegory, it does not require any objective belief in the existence of angels and demons, but the Puritans, whose religion was centered in a way of life, were as keenly aware of the forces of evil as were their medieval ancestors. Of the good angels they seem to have thought little. Across the Atlantic from Bunyan's England, the president of Harvard College, Increase Mather, apparently felt called upon to give instruction on this subject to the people to whom he preached. Near the end of the seventeenth century he preached six sermons on the subject of angels. They were published in Boston in 1696 under the title *Angelographia, or A discourse concerning the nature and power of the Holy Angels, and the great benefit which the true Fearers of God receive by their ministry.*[8] Mather declares the work of "Dionysius the Areopagite" to be counterfeit, and declines to take any part in such "wrangling contests" as the Scotists and the Thomists engage in. He also refuses to venture an opinion on the problem of the existence of guardian angels. He makes no assertion except such as he finds explicit in the Bible. What he does state with certainty is that there are such beings as angels, and that God made them all out of nothing. There is no need now, he says, for angels to appear visibly to men, because the scripture is now perfected. It must not be added to, and it is now "sufficient to direct men in all cases whatsoever, that may concern their Salvation and Consolation."

The general effect of Mather's teaching concerning angels, however, is not consolatory, for the sermons are heavily weighted on the negative side. The Puritan misses no opportunity to decry the superstitions and idolatries of the Papists, and while admitting in a vague and general way the benefits that may be derived from angelic ministry, he is far more emphatic in warning his hearers against the deceptions of demons, who may appear as angels of light. He brings the warning home to them by alluding to certain events of which he assumes they are aware in their own society.

"We in *New England*," he says, "have lately seen not only miserable Creatures Pinched, Burnt, Wounded, Tortured by *Invisible Agents*, but some *Ecstatical* Persons, who have strongly imagined that they have been attended with *Celestial Visitants* revealing secret and future things to them which if it should appear to be Diabolical Imposition, or the effect of a hurt Imagination only, or both it may (if not timely prevented) be of dangerous Consequences to themselves and others." This is the only allusion Mather makes to the cases of witchcraft in New England in pursuit of which his son Cotton was actively engaged.

The tone for *Angelographia* is set by the phrase "Fearers of God," which is used in the subtitle of the book. Even though the author gives some examples of apparently miraculous happenings attributed to angelic intervention—incidents of which he must have heard from his English-born parents or when he was a student in Dublin—it is evident that he had never felt the presence in his own life of a heavenly being and does not wish to recognize such happenings in the lives of others. Women, he says, are particularly susceptible to such deceptions, citing Hildegarde, Bridget, and Elizabeth of Hungary as examples, and he follows his statement with the assertion that the ecstatic visions of epileptics and the trembling fits of "that sort of people who of later years have been called Quakers" are also of the Devil. If any of the "Fearers of God" who heard Mather's warning subsequently found themselves in a state of inexplicable joy or fancied they heard strains of heavenly music on awakening, they must have trembled for the safety of their souls and risen to do battle with the devil himself. Mather and his circle represented authority in a society their fathers had founded for the sake of religious freedom. In Puritan New England the angel tradition languished and the shining angel figures were never met outside the pages of a book.

11 / REVELATION AND REVOLUTION

My God, when I walke in those groves
And leaves thy spirit doth still fan,
I see in each shade that there growes
An Angell talking with a man.
　　　　　　　—HENRY VAUGHAN

At no time in the Christian era have the pervading influences seemed less conducive to recognition of angels than
during the eighteenth century. It was a time of magnifi-
cence and squalor, when the established churches were los-
ing their dominion over the lives of the people, when ra-
tionalism prevailed in philosophy and a ferment of political
and social revolution stirred beneath the foundations of existing institutions. It was a time, however, when differences
were tolerated, when religious sects could develop with little fear of persecution, and the cold speculations of deism
could live side by side with the fervors of pietism, in spite
of the mutual disapproval of those who embraced them.
Expansion of world trade, the steady advance of scientific

thought, and the idea of the liberty of man all combined to place emphasis on the outer aspects of reality, while the soul of man was left mainly in the hands of the moralists. Angels still held their place in the liturgies of historic Christianity and were still seen as active agents in the distant past as recorded in the scriptures, but the story we are following now turns to pioneers in the inner world of man.

Standing out in contrast to their background are the figures of two angel-haunted men, Emanuel Swedenborg and William Blake. Swedenborg, the son of a Swedish bishop, was born in 1688, just three years after the birth of Johann Sebastian Bach. "English Blake," as he called himself, was the son of a London hosier and was two generations younger than the Swedish visionary, whose writings he was to study in young manhood. He was born in 1757, the year Swedenborg saw as the beginning of a new spiritual age. Both men were seers—a term more descriptive than precise —but they approached the spiritual world from different directions, Swedenborg through his studies of the natural sciences and Blake with the intuition of poetic genius.

Swedenborg was already a man of importance before his revelations began, holding a highly respected post as assessor of the Bureau of Mines, a member of the House of Nobles, and a consultant to King Charles XII. Blake, an engraver by profession, never possessed much of the world's goods or enjoyed the esteem of more than a handful of friends. Their reputations, however, had one thing in common, and in common with most people who have visions: they were generally considered insane. The older man, of course, never knew the younger, who was a boy of fifteen when Swedenborg died, but Blake immersed himself in the writings of Swedenborg soon after they were translated into English from the Latin in which they were written. Blake embraced many of Swedenborg's ideas, took fire from them, disputed them, discarded some of them, gave the author high praise, and yet declared in *The Marriage of Heaven and Hell* that Swedenborg had not written one new truth, but a recapitulation of all superficial opinions and an analysis of the more sublime ones. Swedenborg gained a following, especially in England, where a church representing his basic teachings was organized soon after his death in 1772. Blake, the engraver, poet, and painter, on the other hand, remained largely unknown for nearly a century, his talents as an artist recognized by only a few, while his poetry, aside from some of the shorter lyrics, was considered so obscure as to be the work of a madman.

Emerson, writing of Swedenborg in *Representative Men*, said that his scientific work was of the highest order and declared *The Animal Kingdom* a book of wonderful merits. "It was written," he said, "with the highest end—to put science and the soul, long estranged from each other, at one again." Writing at a time when Swedenborg's ideas had considerable influence among philosophical-minded Americans, Emerson spoke of him as a sublime genius who had attempted to unlock the secrets of the universe by seeking the meaning of nature as seen in its correspondence with things of the spirit. As long as Swedenborg maintained his position as a scientist, Emerson's praise was unstinted, but in regard to his claims of direct revelation, which came as the result of a severe religious crisis in middle age, he was skeptical and described the writer as in a state of "theological cramp." In Swedenborg's complicated symbolism Emer-

son found, in the end, only another way of expressing outworn truths. He felt that Swedenborg had become the
victim of his own conscience, and that the scientist, who
had written like a poet, had become a mystic who wrote
with the dryness of a moralist.

The crucial experience that brought about the change in
Swedenborg's life occurred in his fifty-sixth year, when he
passed through a period of intense spiritual anxiety that
affected his health. During that time he kept a diary in
which he recorded and interpreted his dreams and the various psychological phases he passed through. In this intro-
verted state he perceived the heights and depths of his nature and judged them in the light of his conscience. The result was a gradual separation from the life that was natural
to him and the eventual sacrifice of his own nature to what
he believed to be the will of God. It was in one way a typical Protestant conversion of the time, similar in kind to the
emotional change of direction experienced by people who
heard the preaching of such evangelists as John Wesley and
Jonathan Edwards, but in a man of such powerful intellect
and imagination as Swedenborg, in whom it came spontaneously, the effects were of a different order.

Spiritual insight comes to people in various ways, according to their types of mind and temperament. Jakob
Boehme's revelations were accompanied by marvelous experiences of the senses, but when he wrote of the truths he
had perceived, the words came directly, as if they had been
dictated. George Fox, the founder of the Society of
Friends, had what he called "openings," in which he received spiritual enlightenment, but he never claimed to
have entered the spiritual world. Swedenborg was one of

those seers who, without offering any explanation or even a description of how the experience occurs, simply state that they live simultaneously in the physical and spiritual worlds and can see, hear, and converse with spirits. When he was asked to give proofs of his claims, he graciously submitted to tests that seemed to show he had foreknowledge of events and could reveal secrets he could have had no rational way of knowing.

Such phenomena, coming under the heading of psychic powers, are often exhibited by mediums whose personal character and intellectual attainments are of no high order, but Swedenborg was a gifted, highly educated man, successful and at ease in any society, showing no signs of mental derangement, yet claiming knowledge of spiritual matters derived directly from intercourse with the souls of the dead.

Swedenborg's angels were not a separate order of beings but human souls who, by a series of progressions, had become members of the celestial realm. His descriptions of the heaven he saw were categorically exact and detailed, as befitted the observations of a natural scientist, but the picture he built up had nothing in common with the heaven of the medieval scholars except its division into three levels or states. Although this son of a Lutheran bishop never repudiated the church in which he had been brought up, it must have been a shock to some of its members to find in his system a sort of purgatory, representing the first state through which newly arrived souls must pass in order to orient themselves in the new life. Those who were in the first state he called simply spirits. There were two higher levels into which they might move when they became qualified. One he called the spiritual, the other the celestial kingdom, and in both, the inhabitants were those who had attained angelhood. Those who were in the spiritual kingdom were characterized by the love which is called charity; the celestial angels were those who "received the divine most interiorly."

Since angels were human souls, they were both male and female, and in spite of the Gospel statement that there is no marrying or giving in marriage in heaven, Swedenborg maintained that the whole man must be male and female, and that a couple who had been happily married on earth became one identity in heaven. The angels had homes, and there is a quaint charm in his description of the abode of the young virgins, who, like their eighteenth-century sisters on earth, had little gardens to tend and occupied themselves with embroidery. They also could marry after they entered heaven, so that they could become completely fulfilled. Since Swedenborg never married on earth, having received two refusals of offers he made, conjugal felicity in heaven must have made a strong appeal to him.

Swedenborg's orderly heaven could hardly have been seen by another man at another time in history. In spite of the highly organized society he described, he saw the freedom of the will as a basic principle of the law of God, in both worldly and heavenly spheres. No one was to be consigned to hell; those who went there did so of their own accord because they were not able to accept the higher way offered to them. Their sufferings were the natural consequence of their acts, and they still had a chance of redemption, for Swedenborg saw no vindictiveness in God's dealings with humanity. He did not believe in infant damnation and the doctrine of predestination, and to him the whole aspect of hell was different from the traditional one, although the devil and the demons were real to him. He found all three persons of the Trinity in Jesus, who was the central figure in his theology.

Even before Swedenborg's visions began, he had developed the theory that everything in the physical universe corresponds to something in the spiritual universe. The kingdom of heaven as he saw it, however, appears less as a prototype of life on earth than as a reflection of it. It is sometimes hard to tell whether he really intended his elaborate descriptions of the life after death to be taken literally, since he also said that heaven is not a place but a state, and that, as it consists of good and truth, it is possible for it to exist in the souls of men on earth. It is clear that he believed with the utmost sincerity that he had been chosen to put his revolutionary ideas before the world at a time when Christianity had reached a low point and was in need of renewal. His sense of mission appears both in his letters to friends and in conversations with persons who became interested in him.

It is no easier to picture this grave and conventional Swedish gentleman as a revolutionary than it is to accept him as a seer. Except for his retirement from a highly successful career as a scientist, there was no outward change in his life. He remained a stable personality, immensely learned, modest, cheerful, and thoughtful of others. He is said to have had a sense of humor and to have enjoyed an occasional game of cards in good company. His biographers refer vaguely to extrasensory experiences in his childhood, and it is reported that his father also had seen angels, but, except for the period of inner disturbance he passed through in middle age, he led a remarkably rational life.

There is no doubt that Swedenborg really saw the visions he recorded. He probably was one of those rare persons whose unconscious minds erupt into waking life, so that the figures such as everyone meets in evanescent dreams became a part of his conscious existence. It is harder, perhaps, to account for the profuse but orderly expositions of the spiritual life that he drew from them. His keen intellect and broad knowledge alone would not have produced the original ideas that lay embedded in his immensely dry and systematic writings. Since these ideas arose spontaneously from an unknown source, he perceived them as the gift of angels. He took with him into his visionary life a scientific respect for what he called "natural law," and through his belief in the correspondences between things physical and spiritual he humanized heaven, bringing the two worlds that had been so far apart together again. By his projection into the spiritual world of what he found in the inner world of man, he took a step toward the realization of the words of Jesus, "The kingdom of heaven is within you."

When Swedenborg's *Heaven and Hell,* the first of his books to be translated into English, was published in London in 1778, William Blake was twenty-one, but it was not until ten years later that he wrote his commentary on it. At what age Blake began his extensive reading is not known, but as he was brought up in a dissenting family, his thorough familiarity with the Bible probably started early. Before he was thirty he had read Voltaire and Rousseau and applauded their iconoclasm while he deplored their reliance on reason, but he also read Milton, Bunyan, and Boehme. His propensity for rebellion showed itself when he was a youth. As a growing boy he had so protested against restraints that his father is said to have been afraid to send him to school, and at nineteen he became a fervent supporter of the American Revolution. He showed his mystic tendency as a child, when he reported that he had on two occasions seen angels.

In spite of his gifts and training in the graphic arts, Blake regarded himself as a poet, and to him a poet was a prophet and a prophet was a revolutionary. All the old established assumptions were to be questioned; the soul of man was to be liberated from the confining tenets of historic Christianity and a new world was to begin. He found it significant that he had been born in the year that Swedenborg had marked for the beginning of the new era. When at the age of thirty-three he started writing his answer to Swedenborg's *Heaven and Hell*, calling it *The Marriage of Heaven and Hell*, he said in the introduction: "As a new heaven is begun, and it is now thirty-three years since its advent, the Eternal Hell revives. And lo! Swedenborg is the Angel sitting at the tomb: his writings are the linen clothes folded up." [1]

By this time Blake had rejected many of Swedenborg's views, especially those concerning good and evil, and had made his own definitions for these opposites, which he called "contraries." "Good," he said, "is the passive that obeys Reason. Evil is the active springing from Energy." He regarded both as necessary parts of a whole, and the play of the opposites he saw as the source of all human

progress. Thus Satan appeared in a wholly different character from the traditional one, though the figure bore a resemblance to Satan in Milton's *Paradise Lost*. In an often
quoted note at the end of a passage on the devil, Blake said,
"The reason Milton wrote in fetters when he wrote of
Angels & God and at liberty when of Devils and Hell, is
because he was a true Poet and of the Devil's party without
knowing it."

Notes such as this abound in Blake's prose works, in
which his ideas led him on from one proposition to another,
sometimes coming to contrary conclusions at different
times. It was not only his conscious thoughts that Blake
explored, but also the human psyche as he saw it revealed
through his own inner experience. He often used old theological terms such as "the fall of man," finding new meanings according to the discoveries that came to him through
his visions. The fall of man for him consisted not in the dis-
obedience of Adam and Eve to the law of God, but in a
breaking up of the original unity in which man existed in
his first state of innocence by one part of the psyche becoming dominant over the others.

Since Blake was a poet, his way of perceiving was
through imagery rather than in abstractions, so that the
forces that he found in a state of imbalance in man became
for him personifications with names. A whole set of mythological characters developed and became activated for him
as if they were autonomous beings. He saw them not as
projections of his individual psychic experience but as representations of the powers existing in the spiritual world,
both within man and without, in the timeless, spaceless real-

ity of which the physical universe is only a part. The great drama of human existence was lit up for him by the power of his poetic intuition and passion.

Blake's visions were avowedly symbolic, and the cast of his characters was conceived on a heroic scale. Among these the Four Zoas, growing out of his interpretation of the visions of Ezekiel, came gradually to occupy a central place in his symbolic narratives. Their metamorphoses reflected the history of man as Blake perceived it according to his own conception of the fall of man and his eventual salvation through reunification of the disjointed and warring parts. He found the greatest value in the wholeness rather than the perfection of man. Although Swedenborg's idea of the union of man and woman in a single soul did not satisfy him, Blake held that man to be whole must contain his counterpart, which in recognition of the creation of Eve he called man's "emanation." Thus female figures appear and play their ambiguous parts in the whole complex drama.

Since it was around such symbolic characters, spontaneously conceived but developed imaginatively, that Blake wove his immense narratives, his idea of angels was entirely different from that of Swedenborg. His angels were rarely the principal actors in his scenes but were ancillary figures fulfilling various purposes, usually related to the mood or feeling of the events taking place. Contrary to Swedenborg's view of angels as human souls, Blake's was of angels like those of tradition, a separate order of creation. His theme was the soul of man, and all else was used as it fitted his purpose in developing the theme. In a time when reason was held to be the only reliable faculty of man and imagination was decried as "fancy," Blake was drawn into an exploration of the unconscious depths of the psyche. Some of the religious mystics of the past had seen similar visions but had attributed them to the direct influence of God or the devil. Blake was a pioneer in recognizing them as manifestations of the inner world of man. He was, at least in his perceptions, a forerunner of the depth psychologists whose work was hailed as something new a hundred years after his death. Since he had no criterion for judgment when he tried to interpret his visions, his conclusions may often have been out of balance or contradictory, but, taken as a whole and in spite of many variations, the grand design that he projected follows the theme that traditional Christianity labeled "sin and salvation."

Just where Blake's angels fit into the over-all pattern of his thought is not easy to say, for no single definition would cover all the uses he made of them. In an early work, *All Religions Are One*, he associated them with the poetic genius, "which by the Ancients was called an Angel & Spirit & Demon." In the comments he wrote at about the same time on Lavater's *Aphorisms* he said, "Every man's leading propensity ought to be called his leading Virtue and his good Angel." In the *Songs of Innocence*, which represent the state of man before the Fall, they play the appropriate and traditional role of guardians. In the *Songs of Experience*, the angel who takes the leading part in a poem about a maiden queen flees from the girl of whom he is the guardian because he finds her unable to see him except as comforter of her woe and unwilling to accept the gift of love that would lead her into true womanhood. When he returns, it is too late. The prevailing moral restrictions have hedged her in "with ten thousand shields and spears." In "William Bond" the angels of providence, who came with "a black, black cloud," are seen in a complete reversal of the role played by the guardian of the maiden queen. Here they represent conventional morality with its appeal to the sense of duty, while the fairies whom they drive away are the bringers of love.

The role of the angel becomes still more confusing in *The Marriage of Heaven and Hell,* in which Blake put together in a series of poems, aphorisms, and "Memorable Fancies," a framework for his philosophy as it had developed up to that time. In this the angels have become the guardians of the good, which Blake equates with passivity, but the devil, instead of being the author of evil, represents the principle of energy. Not only are the angels on the side of conformity, but conventionally good human beings are counted as angels. It is to the devil, therefore, that the writer looks for creative inspiration. The angels are governed by reason, while at the center of life is found the devil's province, in which natural energy is eternal delight and the source of all progress.

Blake's revolt against the accepted theological views of his time reaches its peak in *The Marriage of Heaven and Hell.* To him, revolution was the third state in man's development, and a necessary one following those of innocence and experience. "As I was walking among the fires of Hell," he said, "delighted with the enjoyments of Genius, which to Angels look like torment and insanity, I collected some of their proverbs." The Proverbs of Hell reflect the wisdom he attributes to his discovery of the principle of energy, which has been suppressed in the name of moral law. Among the proverbs we find such maxims as "Drive your cart and your plow over the bones of the dead," and "Prisons are built with stones of Law, Brothels with bricks of Religion"; but we also find such observations as "The bird a nest, the spider a web, man friendship," and "The cistern contains: the fountain overflows."

In one of his "Memorable Fancies" Blake pictures an angel and a devil in a debate in which the devil proves to the angel that Jesus Christ acted not from rules but from impulse. The passage concludes with this note: "This Angel, who is now become a Devil, is my particular friend; we often read the Bible together in its infernal or diabolical sense, which the world shall have if they behave well. I have also The Bible of Hell, which the world shall have whether they will or no."

The shifts of meaning that occur in Blake's use of the angel symbol do not necessarily reflect successive changes in the development of his concepts, for the angel was for him an inclusive symbol for anything that has to do with the timeless world of the spirit. Albion, the character around whom several of his dramas center, and who stands for man in general and for Blake's beloved England in particular, was himself "The Angel of the Divine Presence" before the Fall, but at the same time "Albion's Angel" was a separate being, taking an active part in *America* and *Europe*, prophecies inspired by the American and French Revolutions.

In the texts where they appear, Blake's angels often remain shadowy presences, mere voices amid the confusion of symbolic happenings. It is in the illustrations and separate paintings that they come to life, as the artist's power of visualization gives them form. Even here they do not appear as individuals, for they are often used as decorations, yet they always occupy space as three-dimensional figures, seeming to float in air. In the Biblical scenes their character is true to the feeling of the occasion as related in the text. The angels on Jacob's ladder are lightly sketched in a receding perspective on the spiral stair that winds upward toward the sun. All are in motion. Some have wings, some not; some carry books, which in Blake's symbolism represent the law; some carry scrolls, which he used as a symbol for spontaneous expression.

Some of the angels of the Bible in Blake's paintings are powerful figures, such as the one who rolled away the stone from the tomb of Jesus. He is seen from within the tomb, his back to the viewer, with wings upraised and arms extended as if in adoration or praise. An angel at the head and another at the foot of the place where the body had lain are folding the winding sheet, which appears continuous with the draperies that clothe them. The merging of figures and drapery which is characteristic of Blake's angels gives them, in spite of the careful modeling, an incorporeal quality, so that the impression is that of a spirit taking form before the eyes.

Blake, like Swedenborg, admitted sex into the spiritual world; it was consistent with his system of universal "contraries" that there should be feminine as well as masculine types among the celestial beings, though they are shown quite as often without any such distinction. It seems to have been the function they performed that determined the way he portrayed them. A variety of types appears in the illustrations for *The Divine Comedy*, *Paradise Lost*, and *The Pilgrim's Progress*. The angel in the *Purgatorio*, whose wings form the sails of a boat approaching the island, is young and strong and fair. The one who sits at the gate as Dante and Virgil start their climb up "the seven-story mountain" wears a long beard and resembles Jehovah in the illustrations for the Book of Job. The angels in *Paradise Lost* follow closely Milton's descriptions. Satan and his host are manly figures, wingless except when Satan enters the Garden of Eden with the serpent wound around his body. Michael is a bearded warrior, and Raphael's quality of gentle benevolence is expressed by a figure of almost feminine grace and charm. In contrast to the definite distinctions among the angels in the illustrations of books, those that appear in the borders and headings of the etched pages of poems, where the connection between the text and the decorations is sometimes tenuous, are scarcely distinguishable from other spirits that people the world of the artist.

In the illustrations for the Book of Job, the most famous and the latest of Blake's completed works, the symbolism is consistent throughout the series, and the angels take an active though secondary part in many of the scenes of the drama. They are sympathetic observers of all that occurs; they weep or rejoice; they mediate between Job and his God, presenting his good deeds before the throne; they push upward in a terrified crowd on either side of Jehovah as Satan charges down to afflict Job, and look on with awe as he is cast out of heaven. In the lightly drawn borders the lines of their figures express the feeling that distinguishes each episode. In some instances they appear strangely independent of the central divine presence, as if they were not creations of Job's God but owed allegiance only to the eternal truth that lies behind the personal religious drama that is the theme of the picture.

Since Blake's interpretation of the Book of Job shows the whole action taking place within the soul, it is appropriate that the title page should be decorated with the figures of the seven "Angels of the Presence," a group that took a definite and special place in the system of his thought. He identified them with the seven angels who stood before the face of God in the Book of Revelation, and with the seven eyes of God mentioned in the prophecy of Zechariah. He gave each a name, all of them except the first being Hebrew words denoting some aspect of God. Each was associated with a special phase in the development of the soul. They represent not persons but states of being, as Lucifer, the first of the seven, tells Milton in Blake's long poem that bears the poet's name. Although in the drawing there is nothing to distinguish them from one another, the names Blake gives them when they appear in *Milton, The Four Zoas,* and *Jerusalem* show that they represent in succession the aspects of God that dominate the thinking of the individual in each of the states of his soul. Starting from a state of unawakened innocence, which is characterized by self-centeredness, the soul progresses through successive states of destructiveness, the first awareness of guilt, the imputing of guilt to others, bewilderment at the terrors of justice, and the coming of morality through the recognition of the law. The last angel he calls Jesus, in whom all the past is wiped out and a new spiritual state is inaugurated.

The title page of Job shows all the angels as conventionalized figures forming slightly more than a half-circle across the lower part of the page. The sense of movement, always strong in Blake's drawing, is carried out here by the direction of head and wings, the whole design forming a sweeping line that passes downward from the right, across the bottom and upward to the left. The last angel is shown with wings pointing up and face averted, as if he were looking at something beyond the sight of the observer. Like Swedenborg, Blake saw Jesus as the whole or universal man, the goal of all the partial and unsuccessful attempts made by the growing psyche in its earlier strivings.

Blake's angels are quite distinct from the mythological characters to whom he gave names. They appear as guardians of innocence and of childhood; they correspond to the genius or the daemon of antiquity; they are the agents that usher in the new, yet, suddenly reversing themselves, they become at times the supporters of conformity. They are present as an accompaniment to the action, like the Greek chorus, reflecting or revealing the feeling of the scene that is taking place. In the seven Angels of the Presence they become almost abstractions, representing different aspects of God, yet at the same time they appear as guardians to guide the soul through the stages of its earthly journey. However varied their functions may be, they represent something that is apart from humanity, as angels have always been. Hovering above or alongside, they are close and sensitive to all the reactions of the human beings they accompany, yet they are detached and of another substance, fulfilling in a new way their ancient calling as mediators between the spirit of man and the mystery of the eternal.

12 / THE BLURRED IMAGE

The angels keep their ancient places,—
Turn but a stone and start a wing!
'Tis ye, 'tis ye, your estranged faces
That miss the many-splendoured thing.
— FRANCIS THOMPSON

Looking back on the arbitrary division of time we call the nineteenth century, we are apt to see it as occupied chiefly with matters of empire and industry, of scientific discovery and expansion in all the affairs of material life; but at no time does humanity fail to produce variety. A century that contained such diverse minds as those of Beethoven, whose death occurred the same year as Blake's, of Queen Victoria, Karl Marx, Charles Darwin, and Abraham Lincoln could hardly be characterized in general terms.

There were, of course, certain trends that influenced the lives of most Europeans and Americans. In matters of religion, a powerful new divisive force developed through the application of scientific thinking. Orthodoxy fortified itself against the changes that threatened to dissolve or dissipate its inherited beliefs. The Roman Catholic Church augmented its authority by the promulgation of two points of doctrine which separated it still further from the Protestant bodies: the immaculate conception of the Virgin Mary and the infallibility of the pope. On the other hand, the Protestant world became splintered into a multiplicity of sects that grouped themselves roughly into two camps representing those who adhered to the literal reading of the Bible as inspired scripture and those who by acceptance of new scientific methods of study admitted human history into their interpretations. For most people, Satan had fallen into the background and was held less and less responsible for the world's wrongs, while the theologians debated whether or not the universal principle of evil could be thought of as personal.

Meanwhile, the idea of the angel became more and more detached from its religious background and floated on the sea of sentiment that flowed from the purely secular romantic movement. The idealization of woman as a being of pure and tender sensibilities, which was fostered by the spirit of the time, offered an object for projection of the angel image. It was in the nineteenth century that the term "angelic" was most often applied to women, and conversely the angel was seen as the epitome of feminine grace and virtue. Wordsworth recognized this in the opening lines of a poem composed in 1824 and apparently addressed to his wife, whose name, Mary, appears in the second stanza:

> Let other bards of angels sing,
> Bright suns without a spot;

But thou art no such perfect thing:
Rejoice that thou art not! [1]

As a poet of nature, Wordsworth did not find the angel relevant to his themes, even in his "Intimations of Immortality," in which he referred to the world of spirit only in terms of a dim consciousness of otherness that is gradually lost in the experience of life.

> . . . these obstinate questionings
> Of sense and outward things,
> Fallings from us, vanishings;
> Blank misgivings of a Creature
> Moving about in worlds not realized.

In an age when poetry reading was popular, the two most widely read English poets of the next generation, Tennyson and Browning, both made frequent use of the angel image in a literary sense, especially when the content of a poem was related to a legend or to beliefs held in the past. In Tennyson's "The Palace of Art" he pictures Saint Cecily sleeping, watched over by an angel, while above the arched ceiling of the hall he sees angels "rising and descending/With interchange of gift." The only hint in his work of a personal association with the concept of angels is in a poem he wrote at the age of fifteen, when he had hardly passed the time of Wordsworth's "shadowy recollections." He called his ambitious work "Armageddon," and later revised it at his father's suggestion, to submit it for a prize (which he won) at Cambridge. In it he described an encounter with "a young seraph," who prophesied the coming of "The Day of the Lord." Whether the experience he related was a genuine enlargement of consciousness or a

William Blake (1757–1827), "The Burial of Moses." (Fogg Art Museum, Cambridge, Mass.)

William Blake, "Then went Satan forth from the presence of the Lord," from illustrations for the Book of Job, 1826. (Museum of Fine Arts, Boston; gift of Miss Ellen Bullard)

John Martin, "Satan as Ruler of Hell," from *The Paradise Lost of Milton*, 1827. (Courtesy Harvard College Library, Cambridge, Mass.)

John Martin, "Adam and Eve See Raphael Approaching," from *The Paradise Lost of Milton*, 1827. (Courtesy Harvard College Library, Cambridge, Mass.)

Mary Ann Willson, "Three Angel Heads," c. 1830. (Museum of Fine Arts, Boston; Karolik Collection)

William Morris (1834–1896), "The Annunciation," cartoon for stained-glass window at St. Michael and All Angels, Brighton. (William Morris Gallery, Brighton, England)

Gustave Doré, "Elijah Nourished by an Angel," from *La Sainte Bible avec les Dessins de Gustave Doré*, 1866. (Courtesy Harvard College Library, Cambridge, Mass.)

Paul Gauguin, "The Vision after the Sermon" (Jacob wrestling with the angel), 1888. (National Gallery of Scotland, Edinburgh)

Marc Chagall, "Abraham and Three Angels Looking Down on Sodom," from the illustrations for the Chagall Bible, *Verve* No. 33/34, 1956.

Mauritz C. Escher, "Hell and Heaven," 1960. (Collection of C.V.S. Roosevelt, Washington, D.C.)

Jacob Epstein (1880–1959), "Saint Michael, the Archangel, and Satan," at Coventry Cathedral, England. (Photo: Courtesy English Counties Periodicals, Ltd.)

purely imaginary one inspired by his chosen theme, the lines do express the feeling of a growing boy when he first finds himself face to face with something transcending nature and momentarily identifies himself with it.

> I felt my soul grow godlike, and my spirit
> With supernatural excitation bound
> Within me, and my mental eye grew large
> With such a vast circumference of thought,
> That in my vanity, I seem'd to stand
> Upon the outward verge and bound alone
> Of God's omniscience.[2]

To Browning, immersed as he was in the atmosphere of his chosen country, the angel was firmly placed in an Italian perspective, where he found much of his subject matter. In his storytelling the angels take the parts that would have been appropriate to the time and place where the events are supposed to have occurred. In "The Ring and the Book" Satan is introduced as the cause of misfortunes, and is seen as

> . . . a dusk misfeatured messenger,
> No other but the angel of this life,
> Whose care is lest men see too much at once.[3]

Of the lady whose perfection is being questioned he says:

> No, they must have her purity itself,
> Quite angel,—and her parents angels too
> Of an aged sort, immaculate, word and deed.

The only time Browning expressed any personal feeling in regard to the idea of the angel was in a letter in verse to his friend Alfred Demett, with whom he was moved to share an experience he had at Fano, on the Adriatic coast.

The poem tells how he found there in a small chapel a painting by Guercino, which impressed him so much that he went three times to sit before it. The picture, representing an angel teaching a child to pray, aroused in him a desire for a similar experience of the supporting power of a beneficent presence beyond the range of the senses. He begs the angel to come to him when he has finished his evening ministry to the child, to cover him with his wings,

> Pressing the brain, which too much thought expands,
> Back to its proper size again.

The most meaningful of Browning's allusions to angels, however, is in the introspective poem "Pauline," his first published work, written when he was twenty. The image of the angel is intended only as a figure of speech, a metaphor used to express his attitude toward the gift of imagination, which he feels has saved him from the despair of youth.

> And of my powers, one springs up to save
> From utter death a soul with such desire
> Confined to clay—of powers the only one
> That marks me—an imagination which
> Has been a very angel, coming not
> In fitful visions, but beside me ever
> And never failing me.

Here Browning almost echoes Blake, whose idea that a man's leading propensity should be called his good angel was quoted in Chapter 11.

In nineteenth-century America, where the court of heaven had no more relevance than the court of earthly monarchy, angels became figures of fantasy, not necessarily attached to Christian tradition. Emerson and Poe both used angel figures derived from religions of the East. Poe celebrated the Moslem angel of music, Israfel, "whose heart strings are a lute," and suggested that if he and the angel could change places the latter "might sing as wildly well."

> While a bolder note than this might swell
> From my lyre within the sky.

The archangel Uriel, in Emerson's poem of that name, is found in a somewhat confusing Persian heaven, containing both "the old war gods" and "the seraphs." In this company, Uriel is true to the traditional role he plays in *Paradise Lost*, where Milton calls him "regent of the sun." Emerson shows him as the innovator, thrusting a new and unacceptable idea into an immutable heaven, where forms and interpretations are thought to remain fixed throughout eternity. In a note by the author's son, Edward Waldo Emerson, the poem is described as a "celestial parable," related to a crisis in the poet's own life when he was invited to address the graduating class of the Harvard Divinity School in 1838 and became aware as the talk proceeded of "the shock and pain of the older clergy present." In the discussion among "the young deities" in the poem, of such questions as "what subsisteth and what seems," Uriel's speech "stirred the devils everywhere" and led to his withdrawal into a cloud, when he stated:

> "Line in nature is not found;
> Unit and universe are round;

In vain produced, all rays return;
Evil will bless, and ice will burn."

The poem seems to have been associated with the essay "Circles," of which one of Emerson's biographers, Richard Garnett, said, "The object of this fine essay quaintly entitled 'Circles' is to reconcile the rigidity of unalterable law with the fact of human progress."

Since Emily Dickinson was a personal poet, her angels were equally far removed from Emerson's intellectual archangel and Poe's heavenly singer. Hers were the simple ministering angels of Christian tradition, though they were shaped and colored by her individual vision. She used them most often in the early years of her poetical work, when she was coming of age as both a woman and a poet. In her childhood she seems to have thought of angels as invisible companions, and much of this feeling was carried on into the period of her most prolific creativity. In one of her early letters to Thomas Wentworth Higginson, replying to his questions about her life, she alluded to angels as if they had been a part of her childhood's world, in which there was no clear distinction between the natural and the supernatural. Although she could have been using the word "angels" metaphorically for the good she found in nature, it is also possible that she was expressing literally a child's sense of the presence of unseen beneficent beings.

> When much in the Woods as a little Girl, I was told that the Snake would bite me, that I might pick a poisonous flower, or Goblins kidnap me, but I went along and met no one but Angels, who were far shyer of me than I could be of them, so I haven't that confidence in fraud which many exercise.[4]

The Dickinson angels are close to human beings, watching over them in their dangerous moments, consoling the troubled, bringing gifts, mourning over the death of flowers, assisting dying souls and conducting them to heaven. They include under their protection the tiniest flower on the lawn, yet in the spiritual world they celebrate the triumph of victorious souls.

> We trust in plumed procession
> For such the angels go –
> Rank after Rank, with even feet –
> And uniforms of Snow.[5]

She seldom sees the angels as majestic, but rather as tender and understanding in their active ministrations to the human souls under their care. Unable to conform to the religious beliefs current in her own environment, she seems to have found in the traditional angels all that was most comforting in the faith she could not accept. She saw them at work everywhere in human affairs. In a poem beginning "Good night! Which put the candle out?" the light that had marked the relation between two persons had been the work of the angels:

> Ah, friend, you little knew
> How long at that celestial wick
> The Angels – labored diligent –[5]

In "A wife at Daybreak I shall be," a poem in which the image of a maiden on her wedding night expresses the feeling of a soul preparing to meet eternity, the angels "bustle in the hall" while her "future climbs the stair."[5]

In her later years Emily Dickinson used the angel image chiefly in figures of speech. In two poems about robins she identified the heralds of spring with Gabriel, and to kill a bird, she declared in a poem beginning "His Bill is clasped, his Eye forsook—" is like firing on angels in heaven.[5] Her early sense of the omnipresence of angels appears again in a quatrain written three years before her death, but this time they are seen as symbols of transcendence rather than as active agents of divine love.

> Who has not found the Heaven – below –
> Will fail of it above –
> For Angels rent the house next ours,
> Wherever they remove.[5]

She claimed the angels, however, as agents of her own love in two of her later letters, where she quoted the phrase from Psalm 91, "he will give his angels charge over thee," substituting "I" for "he." In one instance she called them *his* angels, in the other quite openly *my* angels, but in both instances it was she who sent them.[6]

The angel, as an image that could carry lightly whatever meaning of compassion or power she chose to give it, did not belong in the class of what Emily Dickinson called "flood subjects," such as had to do with the essential meaning of life and death. Even lower in the order of importance was the opposing figure of the devil. Aside from one oblique reference to him in which she describes the slow ruin of a soul as "Devil's work," Satan appears only twice in her poems. Unlike Blake, she seems to regard him with complete detachment. Much of her impression of him was doubtless drawn from Milton, as was Blake's, but her presentation is wholly her own. In one poem she characterizes him as a "Brigadier"—a title she also used to describe the jaunty pose of a blue jay. The only poem devoted entirely to the devil makes him an ambivalent figure whose one great flaw ruins an otherwise admirable personality.

> The Devil – had he fidelity
> Would be the best friend –
> Because he has ability –
> But Devils cannot mend –
> Perfidy is the virtue
> That would he but resign
> The Devil – without question
> Were thoroughly divine.[5]

This attitude toward the traditional author of all evil, characteristic as it is of her special mind, is not without relation to the popular view of her time, when the personal devil had gone into obscurity behind the screen erected by believers in the innate goodness of man and the inevitable progress of civilization.

Since Satan had become a historical figure rather than a force, and the angels as messengers of God were correspondingly dimmed, church art produced little that was new, but fell back on the imitation of earlier styles. The stained-glass angels in the nineteenth-century Gothic churches were seldom more than dim reminders of their prototypes, possessing little life of their own. In the churches of most Protestant denominations, angels were not represented at all but remained firmly shut within the pages of the Bible.

Improving methods of reproduction brought in an immense quantity of illustrated books, both current literature and great works of the past. Fine illustrated editions of the Bible were printed, or volumes consisting wholly of plates illustrating Biblical scenes. John Martin of England produced such a volume in 1835, and the immensely popular Bible pictures of Gustave Doré of France were published in 1866. Both artists also illustrated *Paradise Lost,* and Doré made a series of illustrations for Dante's works. Martin's intensely romantic conceptions of heaven, hell, earth, and Paradise make their strongest impression as entire scenes, in which towering rocks, lightning-pierced clouds, and vistas of immensity in space almost overwhelm the figures. His strong blacks and whites provide opportunity to show the angels as shining white figures, often seen with their wings, even in repose, folded together straight above their heads, like those of a butterfly.

Doré's facile drawing of the human figure led him to give his angels a realism that makes them more earthly than celestial. In the scene in which Elijah in the wilderness is nourished by an angel, a heavenly being is seen descending to earth with a jug of water under one arm and a loaf of bread under the other. His angels are all of one type, a sort of composite rendering of the traditional figures of medieval art, yet in a style unmistakably of his own time. A concession is made to their spiritual nature by the use of finer lines in the drawing than those used for the human figures, which achieves a certain lightness, as of something seen in a vision.

Visions, however, were regarded by most educated people as something that occurred only in cases of mental disorder, though in some church circles those that had happened in the distant past were acceptable. The Roman Catholic Church still allows for the irrational, but the most famous vision of the nineteenth century, which took place at the grotto of Lourdes, was a visitation not of angels but of the Holy Mother, whose elevation had been enhanced only four years earlier in 1854 by the promulgation of the doctrine of her immaculate conception. That, among non-Catholics, the longing for some form of contact with the spiritual world had not been erased by the discoveries of physical science is shown by the popular interest in such phenomena as mind-reading and spiritualism. The latter movement, which may have been influenced by the writings of Swedenborg, originated in the United States and at one time claimed an enormous number of adherents. In its popular form, the religious content of the cult was less important than its demonstrations, and it contained little of Swedenborg's ideas of the Christian life as revealed to him in his visions of the human souls who had become angels. In America, where a society that was being built by the independent efforts of each of its members fostered the growth of many new ideas, some strange forms of religious belief sprang up. Perhaps the most remarkable of these faiths, which became a part of the secular as well as the religious history of the country, was said by its founder to be the result of revelations made to him by an angel.

When young Joseph Smith encountered an angel at Palmyra, New York, in 1823, his visions were accompanied by the aura of light characteristic of angelic appearances. He did not think of his visitor, however, as a member of a separate order of beings, but was never in doubt that he was seeing a human soul who had become an angel on entering heaven. The angel Moroni revealed himself as a member of a people of Hebrew descent who had emigrated to America long before the Christian era. As the last of his race, in the fifth century A.D., he had been charged with the safekeeping of the records of his people, and he had now been sent to reveal the hiding place of the gold plates which he had buried shortly before his death. These plates, engraved in a language Smith called "Reformed Egyptian," together with the "Urim and Thummim" buried with them, by means of which the uneducated youth was able to translate the text of the Book of Mormon, formed the basis for the entire structure of Mormon belief. As a boy Smith had been greatly troubled by the claims of competing sects during the revivals in his small town, but he found a solution when in his first vision, at the age of fifteen, he was assured that he was to found a church of his own. Whatever the source of his inspiration may have been, there is little doubt that he held a burning conviction of his own calling, based on what he considered visible and tangible proofs. Having built up in a few stormy years a remarkably successful theocratic society of followers, he died a martyr to his cause at the age of thirty-nine. The wingless and manly figure of the angel Moroni stands in gold atop the spire of the temple at Salt Lake City as the presiding genius of the now peaceful and effective way of life of the Latter Day Saints.

For Mary Baker Eddy, the founder of Christian Science, there were no material manifestations of angel presence. She rejected the idea of beings with feathered wings and human bodies, saying, "Pictures which present disordered phases of material conceptions and personalities blind with animality, are not my concept of angels. What is the material ego but the counterfeit of the spiritual?" [7] To her angels were not beings of another order but the ideas themselves that were given to men by God; yet she admitted that if she were to represent an angel, it would be in the form of a woman. The truth behind the angel concept was personified for her not in a masculine Logos figure, as in the writings of Philo and the Book of Wisdom, but in the figure of a woman representing the feminine element in the Father-Mother-God. Her views would have fitted well with the popular sentiment of her time, but for reasons other than theological.

The various uses to which the angel image was put in the scattered instances we have looked at in this chapter make one wonder whether the idea of the angel was evaporating in the air of nineteenth-century individualism. Although Catholic children, and to some extent those of other traditional churches, were still taught that their guardian angels saw all they did by day and protected them by night, it is true that in general angels were taken less and less seriously. Thought of chiefly in terms of the past, they had come to occupy in the popular mind a position somewhat similar to that of the gnomes and fairies of folklore. In the use of angels as symbols, however, a trend is discernible in which the pure spirits formerly seen as separated from man by their sinlessness were becoming carriers of a variety of human values. Since astronomical discoveries had dissolved the dome of the sky into infinite space, heaven was no longer a place but an abstraction, and since the earth had been reduced to a minor planet, earthly creatures had been thrown back upon themselves as the only certainty they could grasp.

The humanizing process that had been developing since the Renaissance reached a peak in the nineteenth century.

The scientific exploration of man's psyche had hardly begun, but his environment and his condition became all-important. Christianity was seen chiefly in its humanitarian aspect, and social evils were attacked as problems of material welfare. The age of plush and steam ran the gamut from gross materialism to purest idealism, kept in balance by middle-class conformity. In spite of intellectual and practical advances, however, man still needed symbols by which to represent the inexpressible: such happenings in the psychic life as are only dimly grasped by the conscious mind. In spite of metamorphoses and distortions, the basic idea of the angel, the link between two worlds, remained in the recesses of memory, ready to be re-created with new values according to the needs and the insights of a new age.

13 / WHEELS OF CHANGE

I turn my transient eyes without and see
The world's great ghostly wheels of change reduce
Our mortal home to essences eternal—
The terror and the grandeur, all within.
                    —CORNEL ADAM LENGYEL

The more man learns about the universe around him, the more aware he becomes of the mysteries for which he has as yet no explanation. He has learned to use forces which in the time of his grandparents were not known to exist, but each new field of knowledge that opens before him produces a whole new series of questions. This is quite as true in the sciences that concern man himself as in the fields of physics or astronomy. Psychologists of every school, for instance, recognize the action of intuition and have observed some of its results, but who can provide a rational explanation of the process that has taken place? Who can say with any surety exactly what happens when an extra-sensory experience occurs? After careful observations and the use of apparatus for testing, psychologists have declared that dreaming is an important phenomenon in relation to psychic health, but do they know much more about how a dream is produced than does the primitive man who believes that in dreams his soul leaves his body and actually wanders in another world?

It is only possible, after all, to discuss these phenomena in terms of symbols. We can say that it is the unconscious mind that produces the dream, or that a waking vision is projected by the imagination in response to an emotional disturbance, but the words we use are themselves symbols that only describe events in an infinitely complex but nonmaterial structure which we may call the psyche or soul, and which is not identical with the nerves and brain cells through which it operates. Since there is something in the human soul that cannot be controlled by reason, much that is vital to us can be perceived only in symbolic form. The idea of the angel seems to be as indispensable to the Western man of modern times as it was to his ancestors, even though his attitude toward it has changed.

In the midst of the complexity of new ideas stirring beneath the highly polished surface of life in the early years of the twentieth century, it is surprising to find a preoccupation with the angel symbol cropping up in literature with new vitality. Among hundreds of book titles containing the word "angel" listed in library catalogues, a large number were published between 1890 and 1925. The uses to which the symbol was put were varied and by no means traditional, for by this time every man's fancy produced an image of its own. Often the word was used simply as a figure of speech, standing for a person, an influence, or an abstract idea. This period was the heyday of the figurative angel.

There were also many books containing angels as characters who played a part in the action of the story according to the desire of the author. There was a tendency to treat them with a light touch as whimsical or lovable beings, such as those whom James Stephens portrayed in *The Demi-Gods*. His three heavenly visitors, all of whom have Celtic names, are, for all their superior wisdom, quite as much influenced by the Irish tramps with whom they travel as human beings are by them. Since they own no property, they are able to accept readily the moral standards of those earth-dwellers for whom petty thievery is a way of life. A moral code based on property rights is thus slyly attacked and disposed of in the interest of personal freedom. Stephens' fantasy has the warmth and earthiness characteristic of the Irish imagination, in which the natural and supernatural live happily together and a gentle tolerance reconciles the conflicting passions of human beings.

In Paris, Anatole France used the idea of the angel with satirical humor when he raised his voice against outworn creeds. In *The Revolt of the Angels* he cried havoc among the conventions when he brought the guardian angel of a sophisticated young man into the daily life of his ward. Together with other guardian angels who have deserted heaven because existence there is no longer supportable under the despotism of a god who is hopelessly out of date, he seeks to learn all he can of humanity. The adventures of Arcade—the human name of the fallen spirit—become so troublesome to the young man, Maurice, that he is obliged

to reverse the situation and declare himself the guardian of
his former celestial attendant. The latter and his friends
join an aged gardener named Nectaire, who plays the flute
and who enlightens them about the life of the earth by telling them the story of civilization as he sees it.

When the rebel angels form an army and plan to attack
heaven, they seek Satan for their leader and find him now
living in quiet contentment beside the Ganges. Satan asks
for time to consider their proposal, and, after a warning
dream in which he finds himself corrupted by power, he
refuses to lead them, pointing out, besides, that the narrow
and vindictive god whom they call Ialdabaoth, has now soft-
ened toward human life and become kind. His final words
to his companions are, "As to ourselves, celestial spirits,
sublime demons, we have destroyed Ialdabaoth, our Ty-
rant, if in ourselves we have destroyed ignorance and fear."
To Nectaire, who, it now becomes clear, is Pan, he says,
"Nectaire, you fought with me before the birth of the
world. We were conquered because we failed to understand that Victory is a Spirit, and that it is in ourselves
alone that we must attack and destroy Ialdabaoth." [1]

Brought up a Catholic, Anatole France drew the material
for his fantasies from his Christian inheritance, turning the
assumptions of the orthodox inside out or upside down to
express the new values of the age of science. He needed the
ancient image of the being who stands between heaven and
earth to make his point in his personal revolt against super-
stition and bigotry, even though he used it in reverse. His
very French angels, who are both "celestial spirits" and
"sublime demons," not only represent brilliantly his skeptical philosophy but reflect the view of the inseparability of

good and evil that was becoming prevalent among the intellectuals of his time.

The same theme appears in a book by an American writer, James Branch Cabell, but reaches a less positive conclusion. In *The High Place*, which bears the subtitle *A Comedy of Disenchantment*, the scene of which is laid in the imaginary land of Poictesme, Cabell brings the archangel Michael into a story that wears the mask of a typical fairy tale. The adventures of Florian, first seen as the ten-year-old son of a seventeenth-century duke, carry him through the various stages of life to his thirty-sixth year, but in the end the events prove to have occurred only in the child's dream. Of power equal to that of Michael is another character called Janicet, obviously an incarnation of Satan. As Florian awakes from his complicated and disenchanting dream-life, he sees the faces of Michael and Janicet merge into one. He has learned that his adventures had no moral and that one must not ask too much of life.

The Revolt of the Angels was written shortly before the First World War, *The High Place* was written soon after it, and while such books as these reflected the views of an intellectual minority who were sensitive to the trends of the time, people in general still reacted basically to life's problems and its terrors as human beings have always done. During the years of Europe's great suffering in the war of 1914–1918, spiritual hunger among the men on both sides, who were living in the mud of the trenches and facing death every day, brought angels again to the fore in their ancient character. The need for something miraculous to give meaning to the bleak prospects of reality, the need for help from a power greater than oneself, and the need for beauty in a world made hideous by the destruction of its natural features all contributed to an atmosphere in which visions flourished.

In the early months of the war a writer in London, Arthur Machen, wrote a series of sketches which were published in the *Evening News*. Although they were wholly imaginary, they were the product of the writer's own deep emotional involvement in the events of the war. One of the first, called "The Bowmen," tells of a soldier who in the midst of a battle remembered the figure of Saint George on the blue plates of a restaurant he had frequented in London. Around the figure was the motto: *Adsit Anglis Sanctus Georgius.* Then he heard a great voice crying, "Array, array, array," and thousands shouting, "Saint George, Saint George!" From this vast army, "like men who draw the bow," arrows flew, and the Germans were mowed down as they attacked.

Arthur Machen's sketches were published in a volume the following year, under the title *The Angels of Mons*, with an introduction by the author explaining the strange results of their appearance in the newspaper. The public had refused to believe that the story of the Bowmen was fictitious. It was reprinted in parish papers and published in pamphlet form; it grew into a legend which became attached to the Battle of Mons, the first disastrous contact of the English with the Germans. Machen himself later attributed its effect to his use of the word "shining," which people associated with angels. The story had come to him as he thought of the men at the front, seeing them as if they were in the midst of a furnace of torment and death in which they were consumed and yet triumphant. "I saw our men," he said, "with a shining about them."

Variations began to appear, and new visions and hallucinations were reported by those who said they had experienced them. The English saw Saint George, and the French saw Saint Michael or Joan of Arc. A German general was said to have reported to the Kaiser that men who fell at Mons were actually killed by arrows. In a London hospital a wounded lance corporal told a representative of the *Daily Mail* that on the retreat from Mons he had seen three shining figures in the sky and that the vision had lasted thirty-five minutes. Later a distinguished officer wrote from the front that he and others with him on the retreat from Cateau had seen squadrons of cavalry riding through the fields parallel to their columns. When they reconnoitered they found no one there.

Arthur Machen felt it necessary to protest against the readiness of people to accept his stories as true, but he failed to take into account the effect on others of the intense emotion that had activated his own imagination. Although he had not seen any shining figures in the sky with his own eyes, he had been able to deal with the events that had shattered the comfortable surface of his world only by taking them out of time and relating them to the inner world of myth, in which the particular is resolved into the universal. Most of his readers were probably still living within the framework of religious tradition, even if they were not actively participating in its observance, for no one can escape altogether from the implications of his native culture. To many who accept and follow the teaching of the ancient faiths, belief in the existence of celestial beings was, and still is, a precious part of their doctrine. The Church of England and its American counterpart, the Protestant Episcopal Church, celebrate the feast of Saint Michael and All Angels, and to those who take the liturgy literally, the adoration of the angelic choir is a joyful reality. The Roman Missal contains a prayer added by Pope Leo XIII, addressed to Saint Michael:

> Holy Michael archangel, defend us in the day of battle; be our safeguard against the wickedness and snares of the devil. May God rebuke him, we humbly pray: and do thou, Prince of the heavenly host, by the power of God thrust down to hell Satan and all wicked spirits, who wander through the world for the ruin of souls.

Many modern churchmen, however, think of the angel as a symbol of the mighty forces of the universe which they conceive of as carrying out the will of God, though they still praise the Creator in the poetic language of the Bible, which is kinder to the spirit than the cool terms of science. Man has no words but those of symbolism in which to express his awe before forces beyond his understanding or control.

In order to follow the changes in the image and the meaning of the idea of the angel, we must look outside orthodox circles. With the appearance of the electric light, the telephone, and the airplane, and as if to counteract the materialism that often accompanied them, there developed in Europe toward the end of the nineteenth century a number of esoteric cults derived from Eastern religions. These fostered clairvoyance in their initiates, suggesting to them a universe peopled with spirits as numerous as the angels and demons of the Middle Ages but not identical with them. In England, Madame Blavatsky and Mrs. Annie Besant founded the Theosophical Society, from which groups spread to the Continent. Associated with them for a time was an Austrian named Rudolf Steiner, but Steiner had been a seer since childhood, and his experience led him along somewhat different paths from those of the early Theosophists. Born in 1861 in a small town on the border between Hungary and Croatia, where his father was stationmaster, Steiner spent his childhood close to nature, which he saw with what he later called "second sight." At first he fought against his gift, which set him apart from others; he carried on a normal life and studied mathematics and sciences at the University of Vienna. Extraordinarily intelligent, he seems to have acquired knowledge in almost every field, but his way of perceiving remained unchanged. In his autobiography, which deals mainly with the outer aspects of his life, one finds no amplification of the simple statement that forms the basis of his followers' belief in his powers: "I have always been able to see the spiritual world." What he saw was incorporated into the system of thought he called Anthroposophy, describing it as "spiritual science."

Since the teachings of Anthroposophy are imparted only step by step to those who accept the basic position and wish to be instructed, it is difficult for an outsider to grasp the main points from reading Steiner's works. It is clear, however, that what he saw with his second sight would have been wholly strange to Swedenborg, who was equally certain of the truth of his own vision. Regardless of the value of such revelations as came to these two men, the differences between their views of the spiritual world reflect the differences between their types of mind and between the times in which they lived. Both Swedenborg and Steiner were scientists, trained in the knowledge of their own times, nearly two hundred years apart. While Swedenborg turned away from his earlier scientific approach to devote himself to the purely intuitive path of direct spiritual vision, Steiner attempted to bring the two together and explain one in terms of the other. A photograph of him shows the face of a man so withdrawn into himself that it appears drained of its life, yet Steiner applied his ideas to human affairs, often in practical terms, and proposed new approaches to economics, agriculture, medicine, and art.

It is no wonder that angels took a prominent part in Steiner's vision of the universe, as personifications of the external forces he saw at work on human beings, molding, directing, influencing them, and even struggling among themselves for possession of men's minds. He chose names for these spiritual powers from the religions of East and West and saw them as organized in hierarchies according to their state of evolution. There was an enormous variety among these spirits, which were not, like Swedenborg's angels, human souls in different states of development. Humanity, however, had its own place in the evolutionary scheme.

The archangel Michael reappears in Steiner's system in a new role. No longer the guardian of the Hebrews, the guardian of the Christian church, or the patron saint of a particular nation, Michael is represented as a spiritual power that has a special mission to perform to the bewildered people of the twentieth century. Michael, whom Steiner identifies with the angel of the Lord in the Old Testament, is described as "the countenance of Yahweh, ruler of the night." The truths that came to the Hebrew prophets in moments of unconscious clairvoyance were now to be realized, as it were, by day, through the effect of the spiritual power called Michael. The dilemma of modern man, according to Steiner, was the result of an error made by the Christian church when it declared man to consist of two parts, body and soul, instead of a triad, body, soul, and spirit. This has led, in his view, to the constant warfare between good and evil, for it leaves out the spiritual force that maintains equilibrium. "The Mystery of Golgotha," he said, "signifies the transformation from a spirit of night to a spirit of day." And, in further explanation: "The Word becoming flesh is the first Michael revelation; the flesh becoming Spirit must be the second Michael revelation." [2]

The way of a poet is different from that of a philosopher, even if both receive their impressions intuitively. To Rainer Maria Rilke, a contemporary of Steiner though fifteen years younger, angels were not a part of a system of thought but symbols of a spontaneous inner experience occurring in the midst of an intense struggle with despair. The angels that dominate the *Duino Elegies* were felt, rather than seen, as in an almost overwhelming personal encounter with a powerful force apparently coming from without and wholly other than the poet's own personality. In spite of this difference, there is a similarity between Rilke's angels and Steiner's spirit whom he called Michael, for both offered to man in his dichotomy a third element that would resolve his conflict.

The emergence of the angels in these poems was not as sudden as the force they exerted would indicate. Rilke, who was born in Prague of German-speaking parents, was brought up as a Catholic by a pious mother and undoubtedly became familiar early with the doctrine of the Church. His mother, however, a beautiful but unstable woman, provided a somewhat suffocating atmosphere, from which he was thrust into the rigid life of a military school—a formidable pair of opposites to be met by a sensitive boy. Forced back upon himself, he grew up with only a slight hold on the material reality of the world around him, which he was later to reach for with both hands in his effort to find the meaning of life. His poems mirror the successive stages of his search.

After passing through a period of adolescent atheism, Rilke was moved, by the pious faith he had seen on a visit to Russia, to write a series of poems that marked the beginning of his challenge to the God who failed to reveal himself to him. In *The Book of Hours*, in which the separate poems are really parts of a whole, he wrote at first of a God who is close to man. Then, in an inward journey that took him deeper into his own being, the creative act seems to have preceded the thought, and he found himself seeking a God who was infinitely far removed. In the final portion of the book God still exists, but he is a god of utter darkness, and it is with the angels that one finds the light.

> Where angels dwell, so far was I,
> where light dissolves away so high—
> but God is darkness deep.[3]

These are the angels of tradition, a separate order of beings between God and man, but nearer to man than to God, Rilke intimates, since he represents them as seeking God themselves and striving "to learn" him "from each radiancy." Addressing the dark God and speaking of the angels, he says:

> But I, whenever aught of you I write,
> find they avert their faces out of sight
> and from your mantle's folds too nimbly fly.[3]

He pictures God as an immense tree, around whose topmost branches the angels blow like the wind.

> There in the light they much prefer
> to trust, than God's black night;
> 'twas to their haunts that Lucifer
> for refuge took his flight.[3]

Like Blake, he finds himself on the side of the devil, whom he calls "time's bright god." Angels and devil together have departed from their creator, who is left behind, withdrawn and hidden, obsolete.

To find a foothold, Rilke turned to objective reality, and many of the poems of the next period have to do with his observations of life and of things in the world around him. In verse he was working consciously to develop his craft, while he poured out in prose in *The Notebooks of Malte Laurids Brigge* the tensions that gripped him within. Angels figure in some of the poems, but they are the angels of art as he saw them in the stones of Paris and Chartres. He wrote of the impartiality of the smiling angel with a sundial, to whom all hours are alike, and of another angel figure with head slightly bowed, who seems to absolve himself "from things that limit and direct," for "the eternal future moves through his heart." In spite of the angel's seeming remoteness, however, the poet's view of him foreshadows the coming of the angels of the *Duino Elegies*. In the final stanza of the poem he warns himself (or the reader) not to place any burden in the angel's hands, for the one to whom he comes will be seized and re-created or broken loose from the mold that confines him.

It was in a period of solitude at Duino Castle on the Adriatic that Rilke encountered the angels. When a poem comes from such a deep level of the psyche that the poet feels it has been dictated to him, his symbolism is not a matter of choice, for it is the expression of an otherwise inexpressible experience. The angel is not sought: he comes to him who is chosen, and his coming signifies transformation. After Rilke's long struggle through years of inner torment, in which he sought reality in the visible world, at the bottom of his despair he suddenly found himself confronted by these "almost deadly birds of the soul." Trying to explain what had happened, he said in a letter to Karl von der Heydt, "I regard them as assailants par excellence . . . for when, on my return from a thorough immersion in things and animals, I was looking forward to a course in humanity, lo and behold! the next but one, angelity, was set before me; thus I've skipped people, and am now looking cordially back at them."

The surprisingly light tone of this passage may have been self-protection, such as a person needs to cover an experience not yet fully assimilated, for it was with intense emotion that Rilke wrote of the angels in the poems that were the result of their assault. Probably the best-known phrase in all his work is the first line of the second elegy: *Jeder Engel ist schrecklich* ("Every angel is terrible"). It shocks the mind accustomed to the view of previous generations who saw in the angel only sweetness and harmlessness. Trying to explain the startling phrase to his Polish translator, Rilke wrote, "The Angel of the Elegies is the creature in whom that transformation of the visible into the invisible we are performing already appears complete. . . . The Angel of the Elegies is the being who vouches for the recognition of a higher degree of reality in the invisible. . . . Therefore 'terrible' to us, because we, its lovers and transformers, still depend on the visible." [4]

Rilke had a strong sense of urgency in regard to the task that was placed upon him—the task, he felt, of all mankind —which he thought of as "transformation." One is reminded of Teilhard de Chardin, who twenty years later developed through his fusion of science and religion his concept of man's part in the spiritualization of the earth, which to him was the ultimate goal of evolution. Like many other great artists, in whom the attainment of complete integration as a human being is particularly difficult, Rilke was split within himself between the demands of art and of life. In writing this cycle of laments, he seems to have been seeking release from the tension of the opposites by throwing himself wholly into the world of imagery, which is universal rather than personal, letting one image lead to another as he developed the theme of the unity or wholeness of life and death. In the first flood of creativity, however, the transformation within himself which he had envisioned remained still unrealized. The poetic stream on which he had been carried failed to continue after he had completed the

third elegy, leaving him with unfinished passages for others
which he was not to incorporate into the final series until
life brought him back to the work ten years later. Among
these were the opening lines of the tenth and last elegy,
which point to fulfillment in the future:

> Some day, emerging at last from the terrifying vision,
> May I burst with jubilant praise to assenting Angels! [5]

When Rilke returned to the elegies after the searing
years of waiting during the First World War, he seems to
have found his solution through an identification with the
newly dead. These souls are still close to the life they have
left, but through the new impressions that engage them
they are learning to enter the realm of pure being to which
the angels belong. Even in this life, he intimates, the human
being may find himself fulfilled through submission to the
universal law that governs all things, physical and spiritual.
Instead of the burst of praise anticipated in the opening
lines of the tenth elegy, the cycle ends on a quiet note on
the nature of happiness:

> And we, who have always thought
> of happiness climbing, would feel
> the emotion that almost startles
> when happiness falls.[5]

It is in passivity, the passivity of the dead, rather than in
joyous acceptance of the unity of life and death that the
elegies end.

What, then, is the meaning of those gigantic angel figures
that are so overwhelmingly present in the *Duino Elegies*?
They are majestic and beautiful and always seem to be just

beyond the poet's reach. They challenge him and they possess something that he needs, but their power is threatening. They represent the whole world of spirit, which they bring before him unasked. He addresses them but they do not reply, for the god of whom they are the messengers is still obscured in darkness. They are taskmasters rather than comforters; he does not wrestle with them as Jacob did with his challenger, nor does he call upon them for help. His attitude is best summed up in a line from the seventh elegy: "For my call is always full of 'Away.'" Rich as the elegies are with insights into the human soul, and moving as is the language of their imagery, one feels that these poems leave the "task" still unfinished. The angels withdraw to make way for another symbol that can better bridge the gap in the incomplete circle of wholeness.

In a solitary interlude at the house of a friend in Switzerland, Rilke finished the *Duino Elegies* in 1922. While he was working on them a wholly new series of poems surprisingly came to claim his pen, and in a burst of creativity he wrote all of the *Sonnets to Orpheus*. These twenty-nine sonnets, each complete in itself but following one another like beads on a thread, are closely related to the *Elegies*, but they form a very different pattern. Again the theme is developed through the connection with the newly dead, for Rilke was greatly moved by the recent death of a young girl, the daughter of a friend. He never was able to give to the wholly spiritual angels the jubilant praise he felt was their due, but his praise flowed easily out to Orpheus, the pagan god who belonged to both worlds. Orpheus is the god of the poets, and the *Sonnets to Orpheus* are songs.

> We should not trouble
> about other names. Once and for all
> it's Orpheus when there's singing.[6]

In this group of lyrics Orpheus is a symbol of a different order from the angels of the *Elegies* with their immediacy and power; rather he appears as an image taken out of its ancient setting to form the center for a succession of related ideas, and in no way involved in the struggles of the poet's own soul. The sonnets are far less subjective and personal than the elegies, which were first conceived some years earlier, but it is possible that their spontaneous perfection could not have been achieved if the inner experience represented by the encounter with the terrifying messengers of God had not first occurred. In the shock of this encounter with them the work of transformation had begun.

Strongly individual as Rilke was, he was yet a man of the twentieth century, who suffered from some of the stresses peculiar to his own time. He did not live long enough to meet the bewildering problems of the space age, but already in the first quarter of the century he was a battleground for forces with which the succeeding generations were to strive. The search for identity, which was to become a characteristic motive of uprooted youth in the coming decades, when society was racked by world wars and pushed into ever-changing forms by the developments of technology, led him to look for stability through relations with other people and to try to find himself by immersing himself in the realities of the sensible world. Rilke instinctively sought to achieve wholeness, though often blindly, and his life became a series of experiments that often failed. The assault of the angels was for him intensely personal, but as a poet, whose mission it is to transmute the personal into the universal, he also vicariously expressed the experience of his fellow men.

14 / THE RESURGENT SYMBOL

We shall not cease from exploration
And the end of all our exploring
Will be to arrive where we started
And know the place for the first time
—T.S.ELIOT

With us still, after nearly four thousand years, is the image of the celestial being whom Abraham entertained, who saved Hagar in the thirsty wilderness, who wrestled with Jacob in the time of his fear, and who spoke to Balaam through his lowly friend the ass. The word "angel" is on everyone's tongue and has a hundred uses, but the significance of its derivation is seldom recognized. It is to those who perceive through symbols, the poets, artists, and seekers for meaning, that the angel makes himself known. Sometimes he breaks unexpectedly into the life of a person who is unprepared for his coming, as in the case of the American woman whose vision was recorded in the first chapter of this book, or in that of a contemporary English-woman whose experience is described by Dr. Gerhard Adler in his book *The Living Symbol*. Adler's patient felt herself, like Jacob, engaged in an inner fight with an unknown opponent. When she tried to describe her feeling in concrete terms, she found herself visualizing the power that opposed her as a huge figure looming over her. "Then there formed in my mind," she said, "a definite image of the kind of creature it was, especially the eyes, which were not human eyes." [1] To clarify her vision still further, she drew a picture of a gigantic male figure with wings, who struck at her heart with a bolt of lightning and to whom she had to submit. The obvious sexual association she felt to be only the façade of a much more inclusive experience marking the beginning of an important psychic change in her condition, opening a new phase in the growth of her inner being. Adler wrote: "The patient felt that the angel was something quite new, some inner power never encountered before which carried some message of overwhelming importance." He quotes her as saying that it was a question not merely of submission but of acceptance, and paradoxically the fight was a necessary part of the acceptance. "You know," she said, "that you cannot win but rather that you have to lose in order to win."

Why is this symbolic angel figure so persistent and so powerful, and what is its meaning? It eludes definition and presents so many faces to the inquirer that he is inclined to give up the attempt to interpret it and conclude that the angel is whatever you think it is and in the end may be meaningless.

To the writers of the Bible stories the answer was simple. Everything that happened to man was the direct result of the divine will, of which the angels were the agents. But even in those times celestial beings were seldom encountered by those who wrote about them. As long as man has been recording his past he has looked back to an earlier age in which the happenings in the world appeared to be of a different order from those of his own time. As soon as night has closed over yesterday's events they become colored for each of us with something of our own psychic contents, just as the mystery of the future is filled with our own fears and longings. This is not merely an individual matter, for racial memories grow from the accumulations of individual associations. The senses operate only moment by moment. In regard to angels, how many times has it been said in the course of the centuries that they no longer appear on earth, but that in former times they showed themselves to man? There are few first-hand accounts of visitation by angels except in the recorded visions of prophets or mystics or in the reports of children who perceive intuitively.

We must not forget, however, the unexpected psychic events that can be given the name of "the angel experience," in which an invisible and inexplicable presence is felt. In modern times explorers and mountain-climbers, people of rational and often scientific bent, seem to be most susceptible to such occurrences, but usually they have described the phenomenon only as an illusion caused by their isolation or mental and physical stress, without attempting any further analysis. Francis Sydney Smythe, in his account of the 1933 Mount Everest expedition, gives a clear and detailed description of such an experience. When he was left alone, high on the mountain, he was possessed by the feeling that he was accompanied by an unseen com-

panion. "This 'presence,' " he said, "was strong and friendly. In its company I could not feel lonely, neither could I
come to any harm. It was always there to sustain me on
my solitary climb up the snow-covered slabs. Now, as I
halted and extracted some mint cake from my pocket, it
was so near and so strong that instinctively I divided the
mint into two halves and turned around with one half in
my hand to offer it to my 'companion.' " [2] Smythe's only
suggestion for an explanation was that, as in a fall he had
previously had in the Alps, he was in a state of detachment,
standing aside and watching himself.

This sort of experience occasionally occurs to a whole
group of people. Sir Ernest Shackleton is said to have reported that during his disastrous return from a South Pole
expedition he and his companions were aware of "one
more" who traveled with them, and a Scottish couple who
crossed the Greenland icecap on foot both felt that for a
considerable distance they were being followed by an unseen presence.[3] In such circumstances the invisible companion is almost always friendly, and therefore its presence
cannot be attributed to the nagging fear of the unknown
that sometimes pursues a timid person in the dark, taking
the form of imaginary bogies. If each member of the
Shackleton expedition had been questioned about his individual reactions we might have had more light on the meaning of such experiences than has yet been made available.
As it is, the conclusion can be only tentative, and the relation of the incident to the theme of the concept of the
angel is merely suggestive. All these instances are at least illustrations of the idea of the guardian angel. The failure to
provide an adequate rational answer on the part of those to

whom such things have happened may prove that they cannot be approached deductively. It is not enough to label them illusions caused by physical strain or even an unconscious wish-fulfillment, when they occur collectively. If psychology is to offer an explanation, it must be at the point where it touches the supersensible and merges with the field of religious experience.

Hints of a spiritual world, separated from but close to the sensible, occur among people who already believe in such a separate form of existence. A family brought up in the Church of England, who were gathered at the deathbed of a particularly loved member, became simultaneously aware of something in the room which they could only describe as "like a wind," though the air was still, brushing against them as it passed through. People of the Middle Ages would have called it the angel of death, who conducts the souls of the dead to the other world.[4] A small boy, sent on an errand to his father's study, returned to his mother saying that an angel stood by the door and would not let him pass. After the child's third attempt had failed, the mother went herself and, opening the door, discovered that her husband had died of a heart attack while sitting at his desk. What was the power that protected this child through his vision from the severe shock of finding his dead father?[5]

It is not with the intention of proving that angelic beings exist and carry on a ministry to humanity that these examples of extrasensory experience have been given. If such a spiritual world does exist, it can no longer be considered to be in the sky, but, as Boehme said, "in the innermost of the world," where the visible and invisible interpenetrate each other. No one has yet discovered by scientific methods a location for spirit, though the acts of spirit can be discerned by those who are open toward them. Even in inanimate nature there is a suggestion of powers beyond the range of physical laws, as when a pine sapling, injured by a storm, chooses one of its horizontal branches to replace the broken top and, by changing the direction of its growth, causes this branch to stand erect.

Man as a part of nature lived through eons of time before his consciousness expanded sufficiently to allow him to see himself as separate from his environment. It was then that the era of myth began. With the separation of man from the powers that he saw as his gods, came the distinction between good and evil. The farther a man's aspiration led him toward the light of absolute good, the darker became the shadow of the evil he rejected. Although the human face has been turned more often toward the light than toward the dark, historic Christianity consigned to each individual two angels, one good and the other bad, to account for the predicament in which he was caught between these opposites. For the Christians of the Middle Ages goodness was personified in the good angel and evil in the enigmatic figure of Lucifer, lord of the world and ruler of the demons. Man was left in an intermediate twilight, where Christians learned to function through compensating symbols expressed in the rites of the Church, while Jews found safety in the strictest adherence to the law.

The view that all the events of earthly life were the work of outside forces sufficed as long as the mysteries men witnessed found no rational answers. As modern science came gradually to throw light on some of the wonders of nature, a new form of relation became necessary, but the inner life of the human being seems always to lag behind his intellectual advances, and long-worn habits of thought are not easily shed. Man has hardly begun as yet his task of withdrawing from his environment the parts of himself he has projected into the world around him. Instead he has thrown away much that was valuable in his archaic past and has left himself stranded, in a condition that is neither of the natural world nor related in a new way to the spiritual. He has lost the personal devil who carried the onus of the world's ills, and has placed the blame on his fellow man instead. The average human being has not yet discovered that both the devil and the supreme God are to be met within himself. The heavenly court with its hierarchies of angels, once the glorious background for the controlling forces of the universe, has now become for him only a pretty picture. Since God is no longer thought to sit on a throne in heaven, men seem inclined to think he has ceased to exist.

There are many symbols by means of which man can realize some of the universal truths that lie buried in the deeper levels of his psyche. The angel is only one of them. A living symbol is not invented or chosen, as one chooses a sign or emblem to represent an idea of which he is fully conscious. It presents itself as if it came of its own accord, and it seems to carry on a life of its own. A tree may be a powerful and saving symbol to a person who finds himself uprooted and adrift in a meaningless world. The sea with its depths and its appearance of touching the sky at the circle of the horizon carries many symbolic meanings that affect most people, whether or not they are aware of it.

These are symbols taken from the visible world, though they may have meaning that transcends the physical.

The angel as a symbol is different from those drawn from nature, for from the beginning the concept has been of something beyond the range of the senses. Since no one knows whether or not something corresponding to the idea of the angel actually exists on another level of being, the symbol itself has no such concrete attributes as those of the tree or the sea. Its history, for the most part, has followed the pattern of the kind of God men believed in. Abraham's angels belonged to an autocratic ruler of a chosen people, who sent his messengers to give commands, to protect the faithful, and to exact retribution from the disobedient. The angels of the poets who wrote the Psalms were attendants of a Lord of Hosts and a King of Glory, who loved his handiwork, the earth, who fought for his people and forgave their sins. His angels were "a flaming fire." The angels of the early Christians were the ministers of a merciful Father, specific in their acts of intervention on behalf of men; yet as pure spirit they were subjects of the heavenly kingdom where Christ ruled over the souls of the redeemed.

As heaven became separated farther from the earth, the angels, as the only incorruptible beings in a universe split between good and evil, became personifications of purity and innocence under a God whom it was difficult to approach except through intercession. They formed the background of the heavenly scene, singing praises and attending the triune God, the Holy Mother, and the blessed saints. They were loved and revered as guardians of the soul and adored for their beauty and sinlessness, but were seldom felt as a vital force. If some saintly person became aware of their presence, it was more likely to be through the sound of heavenly music than in a vision.

When the Protestants turned away from images and symbols and depended solely on the word of God as they read it in the Bible, the ministering spirits of heaven receded into the background of memory. Light was focused on the human scene, which was always under the vigilant eye of a God of judgment. If angels were thought of at all, it was in connection with the Bible stories in which they appeared. The great Biblical drawings and etchings of the Protestant Rembrandt portrayed the human side of the scenes as they had never been represented before. Divested of royal trappings, the Virgin Mary as a simple peasant girl received the angel of the Annunciation, who instead of kneeling in adoration before the Queen of Heaven, leaned over her with an overshadowing presence like that of the Old Testament angel of the Lord.

Except where the traditional faiths have continued to foster the ancient views, the concept of the angel has since the seventeenth century been open to personal interpretation. Very gradually a new trend of thought was making itself felt underneath the varied religious developments of the eighteenth and nineteenth centuries. The universe was coming together again, and man's part in it was changing profoundly. From here and there came intimations that absolute good and absolute evil were not forever at opposite poles and that man's mind, in the words of Milton's Satan, "is its own place" and contains the opposites within itself. Swedenborg made his contribution in his statements that man could be at the same time in the physical and spiritual worlds, and that heaven is the conjunction of good and truth in man. Blake's unpredictable insights centered around man as a totality in which the tensions between the opposites maintained unity. While the nineteenth-century conflict between religion and science filled the foreground, the concept of the angel lived on only in obscure or vestigial forms, as if it were a pleasantly remembered fantasy of childhood. It was in the twentieth century that it was to return with power.

In one of Chagall's lithographs, the aged Abraham is witnessing the destruction of Sodom, the city whose sins had drawn down the wrath of God. His three angel visitors are with him, one leading the way as he points downward to the doomed city, the other two supporting on either side the hesitant old man. The ungainly figures of the angels and their not quite human faces convey an impression of an intimate relation with the believing but sorrowful Abraham that binds the four figures into a whole expressive of wisdom, authority, and love inwardly experienced.

A man of the twentieth century, watching with dismay the destruction of parts of his own world, does not see the events with Abraham's eyes, as just punishment for sin. Probing below the surface of consciousness, he has begun to understand a little of the deeper levels of his inner life and to discover how closely meshed together within himself are the evil and the good. A Dutch artist, Mauritz Escher, has made a woodcut, circular in shape, in which alternating black and white figures form a completely interlocking pattern. When one looks at the black, the whole design consists of devils; when one sees the white only, the figures become angels, and the black portions are merely spaces between them, areas of invisibility. In spite of the beauty of the design when seen as a whole, it is frightening when one sees only one aspect of it, whether it is the black or the white that catches the eye. The black figures seem to possess all the energy: the white ones, representing the good, look passive and ineffective in comparison. The design, whether or not the artist so intended it, illustrates man's predicament in finding himself trapped within a circle made up of opposites, from which he sees no way of escape.

Jacob Epstein's gigantic figure of the archangel Michael, on the smooth outer wall of the new cathedral at Coventry, with arms, legs, and wings spread wide, seems to approach the earth with a vigor that is electrifying in its intensity. Arrested in mid-air for the observer to see, the angel of the twentieth century exerts energy from every part of his elongated figure, as if to bring new life to an exhausted world. Below him sprawls the defeated and fallen Satan. The enemy is bound, but he does not tumble headlong into the abyss to burn in eternal flames. He is looking up at the victor with an expression that is more of puzzled wonder than of hate and even suggests the possibility of redemption. Michael's spear is held upright, like a symbol of authority rather than a weapon, and there is no vengeance in his face. His intense gaze is fixed on something beyond the powerful and brutish body of the adversary below him, as if he were about to leap over it to the earth and take part in its life.

If Rilke could have seen this image of the archangel, he might have found in it a representation of the angel of transformation awaited by a spiritually hungry world.

The sculpture carries its message in terms of the time, but the substance of that message is timeless. The figure is not majestic, like the Byzantine angels, or charming like those of the Renaissance. The angel of transformation is sublime, but it is terrible in the sense that Rilke's angels were terrible—as was also the angel whom the Englishwoman met in combat and to whom she had to submit. Unaccustomed to recognizing any power greater than his own, Western man, in his need to find an answer to his contradictions, may be forced to his knees in an inner struggle with the angel of the Lord, who could be the bringer of the missing and saving element.

When a small glowing ember, left among the ashes of a fire long burnt out, is uncovered and exposed to the wind, it may burst again into flame.

REFERENCE NOTES

1. ABRAHAM'S VISITORS

Epigraph: From Psalm 34:7.

1. This experience was told to the author by the person to whom it happened.
2. The legend of Gregory the Great is found in *The Golden Legend*, Caxton's compilation.

2. THE COURT OF HEAVEN

Epigraph: From the Liturgy of Saint James, in *A Treasury of Early Christianity*, edited by Anne Fremantle, New York, 1953.

1. Passages from the Dead Sea Scrolls are from G. Vermes, *The Dead Sea Scrolls in English* (Pelican Series), Baltimore, 1962, pp. 141, 159, 212.
2. The throne-chariot was not merely a product of Jewish imagination. The Assyrians depicted such chariots in the carvings of the palace of Ashurbanipal at Nineveh.

3. INTERLUDE

Epigraph: From William Cowper, "Conversation."

4. THE NEW DISPENSATION

Epigraph: First lines of a Christmas hymn by Nahum Tate.

1. Lines from Robert Graves, "In the Wilderness," *Collected Poems*, New York, 1961.

2. See C. G. Jung, *Von den Wurzeln des Bewusstseins*, Zurich, 1954, p. 175.

5. THE MARTYR'S CROWN

Epigraph: From Bishop Reginald Heber's hymn, "The Son of God goes forth to war."

1. "The Shepherd of Hermas" is found in *Ante-Nicene Fathers*, vol. 2, edited by Roberts and Donaldson, Edinburgh, 1899, p. 9.
2. The dreams of Perpetua and Saturus are found in *Ante-Nicene Fathers*, vol. 3, p. 697.

6. WINGS AND NIMBUS

Epigraph: From Dante Gabriel Rossetti, *The House of Life*, Sonnet LXXIV, "Old and New Art."

1. C. R. Morey, *Early Christian Art*, Princeton, 1942, p. 59.

7. THE AGE OF LEGEND

Epigraph: From "The Lorica of St. Patrick" as given in Newport J. D. White, *St. Patrick, His Writings and Life*, London, 1920.

1. Ibid., "The Confession of St. Patrick."
2. Ibid., "The Lorica of St. Patrick."
3. P. W. Martin, *Experiment in Depth*, London and New York, 1955, p. 241.
4. Aubrey de Vere, *The Legends of St. Patrick and Other Poems*, London, 1895.

8. GOOD AND EVIL IN THE MIDDLE AGES

Epigraph: From Geoffrey Chaucer, "The Monk's Tale," in *The Canterbury Tales*.

1. Caesarius of Heisterbach, *The Dialogues on Miracles*, translated by H. von E. Scott and C. C. Swinton Bland, London, 1929.
2. Sigmund Freud, *Civilization and Its Discontents*, translated by James Strachey, *Complete Works*, New York, 1953, vol. XXI, p. 120.
3. Henry W. Wells and Roger S. Loomis, *Representative Medieval*

and Tudor Plays, translated into modern English, New York, 1942.

4. Dante, *Inferno*, translated by Laurence Binyon, New York, 1938.

5. Passages from St. Hildegarde's *Scivias* found in Frances Maria Steele, *The Life and Visions of St. Hildegarde*, London, 1914.

6. *Meister Eckhart*, a modern translation by Raymond B. Blakney, New York, 1941; Sermon 1, p. 97; Sermon 9, p. 140; from Franz Pfeiffer, *Meister Eckhart*, translated by C. de B. Evans, London, 1924, Sermon XXIX, p. 81.

9. THE CHANGING IMAGE

Epigraph: From Dante, *Paradiso*, translated by Laurence Binyon, Canto 31, line 131.

1. The four quotations from Dante's *The Divine Comedy* are from *Purgatorio*, Canto 2, line 38; *Paradiso*, Canto 28, line 16; Canto 31, line 13; Canto 33, line 142; all from translation by Laurence Binyon.

2. Henry Adams, *Mont St. Michel and Chartres*, Washington, 1904.

3. Julian, Anchoress of Norwich, *Revelations of Divine Love*, edited by Grace Warrack, London, 1901.

4. *The Cloud of Unknowing:* a devotional book by an unknown contemplative monk of the fourteenth century, of which several editions in modern English exist.

10. DIVERSITY OF VIEWS

Epigraph: From George Herbert's sonnet, "Lord with what care Thou hast begirt us round."

1. *Das Handbuch der Malerei vom Berge Athos*, aus dem handschriftlichen Urtext, übersetzt von G. Schafer, Trier, 1855.

2. Zwi Werblowsky, *Joseph Karo, Lawyer and Mystic*, Oxford, England, 1962.

3. Martin Luther, *Commentary on the Book of Genesis*, translated by J. Theodore Mueller, Grand Rapids, Michigan, 1958, Chapter 32.

4. Jakob Boehme, *Confessions,* edited by W. Scott Palmer, London, 1920.
5. Ibid.
6. Jakob Boehme, *The Works of Jakob Behmen the Teutonic Philosopher,* vol. 1, *Aurora,* London, 1764.
7. Quotations from John Milton, *Paradise Lost,* are found in Book 1, line 254; Book 4, line 108.
8. Increase Mather, *Angelographia,* Boston, 1696, "Disquisition Concerning Angelical Apparitions."

11. REVELATION AND REVOLUTION

Epigraph: From Henry Vaughan, "Religion."
1. The quotations from William Blake are all found in *Poetry and Prose of William Blake,* edited by Geoffrey Keynes, Oxford, England, 1966.

12. THE BLURRED IMAGE

Epigraph: From Francis Thompson, "The Kingdom of God."
1. In the Oxford edition of Wordsworth's complete works, 1926, "To ———" is number XV under "Poems Founded on the Affections."
2. Tennyson's "Armageddon" appears in the Cambridge edition as "Timbuctoo," the subject given for the competition, in section "Poems of Two Brothers."
3. Quotations from Robert Browning: *The Ring and the Book,* book 1, 1. 593, book 4, 1.1584; "The Guardian Angel"; "Pauline," 1. 281.
4. *The Letters of Emily Dickinson,* Cambridge, Massachusetts, 1958, letter no. 271.
5. *The Poems of Emily Dickinson,* Cambridge, Massachusetts, 1955, nos. 126, 259, 1544, 1545, 1177, 1479.
6. *The Letters of Emily Dickinson,* letters no. 820 and no. 975.
7. Mary Baker Eddy, *Miscellaneous Writings,* Boston, 1900, p. 375.

13. WHEELS OF CHANGE

Epigraph: From Cornel Adam Lengyel, "In Memoriam: George Santayana," by permission of the author.

1. Anatole France, *The Revolt of the Angels,* translated by Mrs. W. Jackson, London, 1924.
2. Rudolf Steiner, *The Mission of the Archangel Michael,* translated by Lisa D. Monges, New York, 1961, pp. 29, 34.
3. Quotations from Rainer Maria Rilke, *The Book of Hours,* translated by A. L. Peck, London, 1961, nos. 50, 28, 50.
4. Rilke, *Duino Elegies,* translated by J. B. Leishman and Stephen Spender, New York, 1939. Quoted in introduction.
5. Ibid., elegy 10.
6. Rilke, *Sonnets to Orpheus,* translated by M. D. Herter Norton, New York, 1942, no. 5.

14. THE RESURGENT SYMBOL

Epigraph: From T. S. Eliot, "Little Gidding," in *Four Quartets.*
1. Gerhard Adler, *The Living Symbol,* Bollingen Series LXIII, New York, 1961, pp. 205, 208, 206.
2. Francis Sydney Smythe, *Camp Six,* London, 1937, p. 262.
3. See *National Geographic,* vol. 132, no. 2, August 1967, "First Woman across Greenland."
4. This incident was told to the author by the son of one of those present.
5. The story was told to the author by a person who heard it reported as a true occurrence in a sermon in an English church.

BIBLIOGRAPHY

Bainton, Roland. *The Horizon History of Christianity*, New York, 1964.

Baynes, Norman H., and Moss, H. St.L. B. *Byzantium, an introduction to East Roman Civilization*, Oxford, England, 1949.

Beck, Alfons C. M. *Genien und Niken als Engel in der Altchristlichen Kunst*, Dusseldorf, 1936.

Binyon, Laurence. *The Drawings and Engravings of William Blake*, London, 1922.

Blackstone, Bernard. *English Blake*, Cambridge, England, 1949.

Boehme, Jakob. *Aurora*, London, 1656.

————. *The Works of Jakob Behmen the Teutonic Philosopher*, vol. I, London, 1764.

————; edited by W. Scott Palmer. *Confessions*, London, 1920.

Boldt, Ernst; translated by Agnes Blake. *From Luther to Steiner*, London, 1923.

Bornkamm, Heinrich. *Luther's World of Thought*, St. Louis, Missouri, 1958.

Caesarius of Heisterbach; translated by H. von E. Scott and C. C. Swinton Bland. *The Dialogue on Miracles*, London, 1929.

Carol, Juniper B. *Mariology*, vol. I, Milwaukee, Wisconsin, 1955.

Caxton, William. *The Golden Legend* (in modern English), London, 1878.

Dalton, Ormonde de M. *Byzantine Art and Archaeology*, Oxford, England, 1911.

Damon, S. Foster. *A Blake Dictionary*, Providence, Rhode Island, 1965.

Dawson, M. M. *The Ethical Religion of Zoroaster*, New York, 1931.

Delahaye, Hippolyte. *The Legends of the Saints*, London, 1907.

Didron, Adolphe; translated by E. J. Millington. *Christian Iconography*, vol. 2, London, 1851–1891.

Diehl, Charles. *Manuel d'Art Byzantin*, Paris, 1910.

Emerson, Ralph W. *Representative Men*, chapter on Swedenborg, Boston, 1849.

Eusebius Pamphili; edited by William Cureton. *History of the Martyrs in Palestine*, Edinburgh, 1861.

Evans, John Henry. *Joseph Smith, an American Prophet*, New York, 1946.

Every, George. *The Byzantine Patriarchate*, London, 1947.

Ferguson, George W. *Signs and Symbols in Christian Art*, New York, 1954.

Ferrua, Antonio. *Le Pitture della Nuova Catacomba Via Latina*, Rome, 1960.

Figgis, Darrell. *Paintings of William Blake*, New York, 1925.

Finnegan, Jack. *Light from the Ancient Past*, Princeton, New Jersey, 1959.

Gantner, Joseph, and Pobé, Marcel. *The Glory of Romanesque Art*, New York, 1956.

Gardner, Helen. *Art Through the Ages*, New York, 1926.

Gogarty, Oliver St. John. *I Follow Saint Patrick*, London, 1938.

Grabar, André, and Nordenfalk, Carl. *Early Medieval Painting*, Switzerland, 1957.

Guerdan, René; translated by D. L. B. Hartley. *Byzantium, Its Triumphs and Tragedy*, London, 1956.

Heer, Friedrich; translated by Janet Sondheimer. *The Medieval World: Europe, 1100–1350*, Cleveland, Ohio, 1962.

Hinds, Allen. *A Garner of Saints*, London, 1900.

Hite, Lewis Field. *Swedenborg's Historical Position*, Boston, 1928.

Hotson, Clarence Paul. *Emerson and Swedenborg*, Cambridge, Massachusetts, 1929.

Huizinga, Johan. *The Waning of the Middle Ages*, London, 1927.

Julian, Anchoress of Norwich; edited by Grace Warrack. *Revelations of Divine Love*, London, 1901.

Jung, C. G.; translated by R. F. C. Hull. *Aion: Researches into the Phenomenology of the Self*, London, 1959.

Jung, Leo. *Fallen Angels in Jewish, Christian and Mohammedan Literature*, Philadelphia, 1926.

Landau, Rom. *God Is My Adventure*, chapter on Rudolf Steiner, New York, 1936.

Langton, Edward. *The Ministries of the Angelic Powers*, London, 1936.

———. *Satan, a Portrait*, London (no date).

Lewis, C. S. *The Discarded Image*, Cambridge, England, 1964.

Luther, Martin; translated by J. Theodore Mueller. *Commentary on the Book of Genesis*, Grand Rapids, Michigan, 1958.

Morey, Charles R. *Early Christian Art*, Princeton, New Jersey, 1942.

Mowry, Lucetta. *The Dead Sea Scrolls and the Early Church*, Chicago, 1962.

Nelson, Lawrence E. *Our Roving Bible*, New York, 1945.

Peters, H. F. *Rainer Maria Rilke: Masks and the Man*, Seattle, Washington, 1960.

Pfeiffer, Franz; translated by C. deB. Evans. *Meister Eckhart*, London, 1924.

Pfeiffer, Robert H. *The Books of the Old Testament*, New York, 1957.

Quasten, Johannes. *Patrology*, Utrecht, 1950.

Raine, Kathleen. *Blake and England*, Cambridge, England, 1960.

Reich, Emil. *Women Through the Ages*, London, 1908.

Reinach, Salomon; translated by Florence Simmonds. *A Short History of Christianity*, London, 1922.

Roberts and Donaldson. *Ante-Nicene Fathers*, Edinburgh, 1899.

Sackville-West, Victoria. *Saint Joan of Arc*, Garden City, New York, 1936.

Steele, Francesca Maria. *The Life and Visions of Saint Hildegarde*, London, 1914.

Steiner, Rudolf. *Knowledge of the Higher Worlds*, New York (no date).

———. *An Outline of Occult Science*, New York, 1922.

Swedenborg, Emanuel; translated by Samuel Noble. *Heaven and Hell*, New York, 1859.

Trobridge, George. *A Life of Emanuel Swedenborg*, London, 1926.

Villette, Jeanne. *L'Ange dans l'art d'Occident du XIIème au XVIème siècle*, Paris, 1940.

von Rad, Gerhard; translated by John H. Marks. *Genesis: a Commentary*, Philadelphia, 1961.

Watts, Alan. *Myth and Ritual in Christianity*, New York, 1954.

Werblowsky, R. J. Z. *Joseph Karo, Lawyer and Mystic* (vol. 4 in *Scripta Judaica*), Oxford, England, 1962.

———. *Lucifer and Prometheus*, London, 1952.

West, Robert H. *Milton and the Angels*, Athens, Georgia, 1955.

White, Helen C. *The Mysticism of William Blake*, New York, 1964.

Williams, Charles. *The Descent of the Dove*, London, 1939.

Wilpert, Josef. *Die Romischen Mosaiken und Malereien der kirchlichen Bauten vom IV bis XIII Jahrhundert*, Freiburg, 1916.

Woolley, Leonard. *Abraham*, New York, 1936.

Worcester, Benjamin. *Life and Mission of Emanuel Swedenborg*, Boston, 1883.

Yale Reports on Dura-Europos. *The Excavation at Dura-Europos, Preliminary Report*, article by Kraeling on Jewish religious art, article by Rostovtzeff on Christian chapel, New Haven, 1928–1936.

OTHER WORKS CONSULTED

The Interpreter's Bible
The Century Bible, Genesis
Encyclopædia Britannica
The Catholic Encyclopedia
The Jewish Encyclopedia
Hastings' *Encyclopedia of Religion and Ethics*
Hastings' *Dictionary of the Bible*

Langdon, Stephen Herbert. *Semitic Mythology* (vol. V of *The Mythology of All Races*), Boston, 1931.

Some of the books in this list were recommended in conversations with Professors Giles Constable, Krister Stendahl, and Isadore Twersky, all of Harvard University. The author wishes to express her sincere thanks for their cordial assistance.

INDEX